I0620410

Not Suspicious

in Hollywood

Leonie Gant

Copyright © 2015 Leonie Gant
All rights reserved.

No part of this publication may be reproduced,
distributed, or transmitted in any form or by any means,
including photocopying, recording, or other electronic or
mechanical methods, without the prior written permission
of the publisher, except in the case of brief quotations
embodied in critical reviews and certain other
noncommercial uses permitted by copyright law.

This novel is a work of fiction. Names, characters,
businesses, places, events and incidents are either the
product of the author's imagination or used in a fictitious
manner. Any resemblance to actual persons, living or dead,
or actual events is purely coincidental.

ISBN-13: 978-0-9942990-9-3

Dedication

To Ivan, Rob and Ho for inadvertently inspiring me.

Chapter One

Sometimes you have a job that all logic tells you should really suck. I honestly thought my latest job would. Being the personal assistant to one of the hottest rock bands on the planet, five guys who had slept their way through a good proportion of the female population of three continents, should qualify as one of those jobs. Having part of my job description being to take care of the girls who made the questionable choice to partake of the delights of this particular group of guys, was not part of any career path that I had ever imagined myself on.

In the last month I had discovered exactly how the backstage area of a rock band worked and it had been an eye opener. I thought after over a year working in Hollywood that I had been exposed to pretty much every deviant behavior that was out there. My current job proved to me that, despite my pretensions at sophistication, I was still a babe in the woods.

After my initial week working for this band, for the first time in my career as a personal assistant to the most difficult clients, I had been ready to throw it in. I found the guys rude and more annoying than anyone that I had ever met. Considering my line of work, that was definitely saying something.

At the end of that first week though, something magical happened. My boyfriend turned up to drive me home after a particularly long night watching these guys party. Detective Jake Griffin, who had been listening to me complain about the band for a week, put on his cold cop face to greet my newest clients. He put his hands on his hips, showing his badge and gun and stared the guys down. He couldn't have marked his territory more clearly if he had peed around me.

After that moment I became the sexless den mother figure to five overindulged and overpaid men in their twenties. All of a sudden my job became fun, because when these guys weren't being chauvinistic, obnoxious jerks trying to get you into bed, they were a load of laughs. Seriously, if I didn't know what they were like with women, I would have set them up with friends.

My job usually requires me to deal with unusual situations. In this case I was hired by the recording company to keep an eye on the guys that make up Crispy Spider while they worked on their new album. I had previously worked with this particular recording company while dealing with one of their teenage pop brats. The pop star hated me with an absolute passion and had complained loudly and bitterly to his management about how I had ruined his fun. For some reason this now qualified me as an expert with dealing with the excesses in the music industry.

The band was currently sequestered on a large property in Los Angeles where they were working on songwriting and recording. Being a new band the guys had quickly fallen into the rock star lifestyle and had become distracted from the business of making money. The record company wanted me to assist in guiding the guys back into the business side of their job and to try to avoid some of the scandals which had followed these gentlemen through the aforementioned three continents. My job was to try to manage the situations the band got themselves into and prevent them from ending up in the tabloids, or in jail.

My job description had been laid out to me pretty clearly by my boss, Monique Petit, who owned the agency I worked for. She had even sent in my friend, Jorge, to work for security as back up if I needed it. Of course, Jorge was only going to be useful to me if he would stop laughing at the unfortunate predicament I had managed to find myself in.

"Have you finished?" I asked.

Jorge wiped the tears from his eyes. "Wasn't today supposed to be your day off?"

"Yes it was, and if you will help me, it still could be. I have a police function to go to with Griffin and I need you to help me so I can get there."

I could see Jorge was contemplating his next step. Admittedly, I had managed to find myself in a position which, even with my ability to get myself into unusual situations, was a little out there.

I was used to the sometimes unique pets that celebrities had. Mostly they stuck with dogs that could fit in handbags, sometimes there were pigs and I had even had reptiles. The drummer of Crispy Spider had decided his life would only be complete if he had a goat. It wasn't even a little baby goat with that level of cuteness that could make you forget that it was currently destroying a thirty thousand dollar leather couch. No, this was a full grown male goat with big horns and a bad temper. He had been in the house for less than half an hour and had already decided that he didn't like me. I was assuming the reason for that was because I had walked into the living room, seen what he had decided was for breakfast, screeched at him and then tried to pull him off the couch. I was currently standing over him, with each leg on either side of the goat's back, bending over with my arms wrapped around the goat's chest, trying desperately to pull him away from the couch.

"What do you want me to do?" asked Jorge. "I'm a city boy from LA. What do I know about goats? You're the farm girl from Australia. Aren't you an expert in these things?"

"We have sheep at home. Sheep are gentle, dumb souls who will go where you lead them, usually. Goats are destructive forces of evil, only suited to wide open spaces. They should never be in a city, let alone inside a mansion. A pen has been set up outside. I need you to help me get this animal into the pen before it causes any more damage."

Jorge sighed in that way he had started to develop that told me that working with me was no longer such a special experience.

"Tell me what to do."

"Okay," I said, breathing a little heavily. "I want you to stand in front of the goat and hold his horns. Make sure you do it gently. Don't be too rough."

I glanced up to find Jorge looking at me with another expression he had adopted around me lately. "Are you out of your mind?"

I really didn't know why I was copping this kind of attitude today.

"Not as far as I'm aware," I tried to keep a reasonable tone. "The goat needs to be moved and we need to be the ones to move him."

I understood that this would be considered an unusual situation for Jorge. I was trying to be patient. I really was. But I could feel the muscles in the goat bunching up and his movements were becoming stronger. According to my estimation, I had a very short period of time before I was going to be in for a world of hurt.

"Those horns look like they could do some damage."

"Of course they could do some damage." I was beginning to get annoyed. "That's generally what horns are for."

"I'm not really comfortable with the level that those horns are at."

I looked up to find Jorge had crossed his hands over his groin area.

Jorge shook his head. "And I'm really not happy with the idea of me standing that closely to those horns or, for that matter, those teeth. I think it's a workplace safety issue."

Jorge worked security for celebrities. I had never thought that workplace safety was a high priority for him. I would have argued the point but at that moment those bunched up muscles that had caused me some concern previously exploded into action. I wasn't really sure what happened because the next thing I knew I was flat on my back looking up at a goat that I swear was laughing at me. Jorge had retreated behind a high back chair, protecting what was obviously most important to him.

"You okay?" he called out, keeping a wary eye on the animal which seemed very proud of the way that it had demonstrated its dominance over me.

"No. I'm not okay. That hurt."

Jorge did not make a move toward me and I recognized the fact that he had decided I needed to take care of myself in this situation. I rolled over on my front and raised myself onto my hands and knees. The goat bleated at me as if challenging me to take it on again. I really didn't want to but everybody who had a job sometimes had to do things they didn't want to do.

"Got a new plan, cupcake?"

I looked warily at the goat. "We need some rope."

Between the two of us, and with a great deal of colorful language that my mother would have been horrified to hear, we finally managed to get the goat outside and into its pen.

"So the pen will hold it?" asked Jorge, wiping the sweat from his forehead.

"Not a chance," I replied.

Despite my limited knowledge about goats, I had a feeling that this one was not going to stay confined unless it wanted to be.

Jorge looked at me with surprise. "Then why did we just wrestle this thing all the way out here?" he asked.

"We have limited choices," I said. "Either we put it in this pen or we leave it in the house. Putting it in the pen gives us a chance to keep that walking disaster contained, at least temporarily."

"Don't really have a high opinion of goats do you?" Jorge said.

"Why ever not?" asked a voice from behind us.

I turned around to find Vale, the drummer of Crispy Spider and new owner of the goat, standing behind us.

"Exactly how long have you been watching us?" I asked suspiciously.

"Long enough to regret not having a camera on me," said Vale, smiling.

Out of all the guys in the band, despite his appalling taste in pets, I had to admit that I liked Vale the most. He had a shy air about him, or as shy as a rock star could be.

"You could have helped us," I glared at him.

"Where would the fun be in that?" he smiled.

I gestured to the goat. "Well here he is. Have you come up with a name for him yet?"

Vale nodded. "Buddy."

"After Buddy Rich, the jazz drummer," I guessed.

Vale looked impressed. "You know your drummers."

"Actually," I said. "I know you. Believe it or not, I do research before I take on a job and I read an article where you said that your hero was Buddy Rich."

Vale leaned back against a pillar. "So, what else did you find out about me?" he asked.

I smoothed down the creases in my pants which were now covered in goat hair. "According to your press you are a Casanova who breaks hearts everywhere you go. You have an anger management problem and the destruction that goat is going to cause is nothing compared to the destruction you have wrought in hotel rooms across the world."

Vale arched an eyebrow at me. "And what do you know about me?"

"That maybe the press doesn't have all the facts," I said softly.

Vale straightened up. "I think we're going to miss you when you leave us," he said before turning around and going back in the house.

I looked up at Jorge to see an amused expression on his

face.

"What?" I asked.

"I think that boyfriend of yours needs to keep a close eye on you," he said.

"Why?" I asked quizzically.

"You seem to surprise people and they start thinking you're delightful. This can lead to confusion in relationships."

I snorted. "Did you just use the term 'delightful'?"

If you took into account his size and how he scared people by just walking into the room, I had never expected to hear the word 'delightful' coming from him.

Jorge looked at me sourly. "Go, have your day off. I'll see you bright and early tomorrow morning. Maybe the goat will decide it likes you by then."

Considering the way that goat was looking at me, I didn't think that was likely.

Chapter Two

Back at my apartment, I quickly divested myself of the goat infested clothing and had a quick shower. This was the first time that Griffin was taking me to one of the social events that the cops at the station sometimes held and I really wanted to make a good impression. While I was getting dressed I heard a key in my apartment door.

"You ready?" called out Griffin.

"Not yet," I called back, trying to get my hair into some style which looked like I put some effort into it.

Griffin came up behind me, wrapped his arms around my waist and kissed my neck.

"You look ready to me," he said.

I leaned back into him, enjoying the moment.

"I don't want to embarrass myself or you," I murmured, my eyes suddenly unable to meet his in the mirror.

I knew that pretty much all of the people that Griffin worked with were aware of my unfortunate habit of ending up at crime scenes. I also knew that cops being cops, he had been on the receiving end of quite a lot of ribbing from his coworkers, some of it good-natured, some of it not so much.

Griffin turned me around and held my shoulders. He tipped my chin upwards until I was looking deeply into his beautiful green eyes.

"I am proud to have you with me. I love you and I don't care what the others say." He touched his lips gently against mine.

When he lifted his head I smiled back at him.

"What are they saying about me?" I asked.

Griffin rolled his eyes and turned me back to the mirror.

"Finish getting ready. We're going to be late."

I was still not feeling comfortable when Griffin and I arrived at the barbecue. I knew it was something that cops did, getting together to wind down after some tough times. I just wasn't sure why I had to go.

"Relax." Griffin put his hand on my knee and squeezed. "You've met most of the people you are going to be seeing today."

"At crime scenes," I bit out.

I had no illusions about my reputation for discovering dead bodies. Jorge was only too pleased to inform me that the main reason he was the only security person that Monique could get to work with me was because the others were too scared. Griffin's partner, Detective Liza Ramos, was also quite willing to inform me of the stories that made their way around the station. My notoriety and Griffin's willingness to still keep seeing me despite the perceived increased risk of death, did only good things for his reputation.

"You'll be fine," Griffin assured me.

I wished I had his confidence. Even with Griffin standing next to me with his arm flung carelessly around my shoulder, I still felt self-conscious.

"You remember Lieutenant Ellis, don't you, Trudie?" asked Griffin.

I nodded but the lieutenant had that expression which meant that he had no idea who I was. Fortunately, Griffin saw that too.

"Lieutenant, this is my girlfriend, Trudie. She helped us on the Eleanor Channing case."

Of course that was a nice way of saying it. The truth was a little more colorful. It included me being blackmailed for my help when Griffin threatened to have me deported after I accidentally elbowed him in the face. If I thought about it too hard it was a rather worrying start to a relationship.

Recognition bloomed on the lieutenant's face but I

should have realized that it wasn't for me.

"I remember you," he said, smiling. "Interesting case that one."

He paused for a moment and I knew where he was going next.

"Your boss," mentioned the lieutenant with that glazed look in his eyes that I was used to seeing when men were talking about Monique. "Lovely woman."

"Yes," I nodded. "Her husband definitely thinks so."

And there was that crestfallen look again. Sometimes it felt like I was kicking puppies when I broke these men's hearts.

"She's married?" he asked, vainly hoping he had misheard me.

I nodded again. "Yes, to Reggie Goodman, the lawyer that was with us in the office that day."

"Who?"

Griffin's lieutenant looked perplexed and in some ways I couldn't blame him. When Monique was in the room she seemed to pull all the attention towards her. The rest of us mere mortals were ignored. I was used to it.

Lieutenant Ellis wandered off, his shoulders slumped as if the light had been sucked out of his life.

"You had to break his heart, didn't you?" murmured Griffin.

I snorted. "Monique would have chewed him up and spit him out. The only man alive who can handle her is the one she is married to."

"True," said Griffin.

"So, Griffin, you finally decided to bring her," said a voice from behind us.

Aah, I knew those dulcet tones.

"Detective Ramos," I said as I turned around. "Always a pleasure."

"More so for you than me," said Ramos, smiling.

How I enjoyed these moments. I was surprised to see that Ramos was holding hands with a beautiful woman.

"This is Jolena, my girlfriend," said Ramos proudly and I could see why she was. Between Jolena's blonde angelic features and Ramos's striking darker coloring, the two of them looked incredibly compelling and drew attention from everybody at the party.

"Jolena, this is my partner, Jake Griffin, and his girlfriend, Trudie," Ramos said.

"Pleased to meet you finally," said Griffin. "Believe me, I've heard a lot about you."

"All good things I hope," said Jolena, smiling as she gazed adoringly up at Ramos.

"How long have you been together?" I asked, hoping my voice was holding steady.

"A couple of months," said Ramos, looking happier than I had ever seen her.

I went quiet, hoping nobody would notice. While Griffin, Jolena and Ramos kept talking, I stayed silent, hoping to be as unobtrusive as possible. I lowered my eyes as I pressed into Griffin's side, smiling when required but other than that using my ability to blend into the background to as good effect as I could. As soon as I was able to discreetly withdraw I wandered away from the group and found other people to talk to.

At the end of the night I sat quietly in the car as Griffin drove us back to my apartment. I could feel Griffin looking at me curiously but he didn't push. I knew he would. I didn't think my behavior had gone unnoticed and Griffin knew me too well to let it go. To give him credit he waited until we were back at my apartment.

"What's wrong with you?" Griffin asked. "You've been acting strange ever since the barbecue."

"Why didn't you ever tell me Ramos was gay?" I asked quietly.

Griffin shrugged. "It didn't matter I guess. I'm more interested in the fact the woman can shoot on target every single time. What she does in her personal life is really none of my business." He paused for a moment. "Do you have a problem with her being gay?"

"No," I said, turning around and busying myself with some cups. "Do you want a coffee?"

"Stop," growled Griffin. "Something is going on here and I need to know about it."

"It's nothing," I said. "I just thought… No, actually, you're right. Ramos's relationship is completely none of our business."

Griffin stood up, put his hands gently on my shoulders and turned me around. "Something is bothering you. I can't fix it if you don't tell me what the problem is."

"You can't fix this anyway," I said quietly. "If you know, it is going to cause problems and I don't want to do that to you."

"Just tell me," said Griffin patiently as he stroked strands of hair away from my face.

"I've met Ramos's girlfriend before," I said guardedly, watching his eyes.

"Go on."

"To be perfectly honest I've had security pull her out of the bed of one of the guys in the band when a threesome went a little too wild." I said it quickly, hoping the impact would be lessened.

"Hell," said Griffin.

I nodded in total agreement.

"Do you think she recognized you?" he asked.

"I don't know," I said. "She was pretty out of it and hysterical. I stayed back because some of these women have done so much to end up with these guys that they can get violent if they are denied. It's one of the reasons that Monique insisted that Jorge do this job with me. She knows that he would quite happily throw the clients under the bus to protect me. I know Jolena fought Jorge so hard that he had difficulty restraining her without hurting her."

"Did you call the cops?" Griffin asked.

"Of course we didn't call the cops," I said. "You've met the people I work with. Unless there was the threat of imminent death, there is no way that they would call the cops for anything."

"How long ago was this?" asked Griffin.

"Three days," I said. "The way Ramos was talking, she seems to think they are exclusive."

Griffin wiped his hand over his face. "How the hell am I supposed to deal with this?" he asked. "Ramos and I have very definite boundaries. We do not talk about private stuff. Work, sports, current affairs, and how much of an idiot the lieutenant is, pretty much covers our daily conversations. That and what other harebrained situation you've got yourself into. If I tell her about this it could affect our work."

I realized he was under some pressure so for the moment I was going to ignore the harebrained comment.

"If it was me cheating on you and Ramos found out, would you want her to tell you?" I asked.

I saw Griffin's features tighten and wondered if that was the best question I could have brought to his attention.

He nodded slowly. "I would hate that she knew and I would be angry at her for telling me, but I would never want to be made to feel like a fool. I would be mad if she told me but if I found out later that she knew and didn't tell me, I would be furious."

"Then I guess you need to work out what is best for Ramos," I said. I looped my arms around him. "I'm sorry."

"What are you sorry for?" asked Griffin. "You aren't the one who cheated on Ramos and put me in this lousy position."

"True," I said. "I'm sorry because this is a messed up situation to be in. Nobody ever wants to have this information about a friend. There are usually no winners when you tell someone their partner is cheating on them."

"Out of curiosity, which of the guys was Jolena sleeping with?" asked Griffin.

"Ash," I said.

Griffin nodded and from what I had already told him about Ash, I didn't think he was surprised. Ash Weston was the lead singer of Crispy Spider. While I had grown fond of the other members of the band, I usually kept my distance from Ash. He had an edge to him which gave me a bad feeling and I was a great believer in listening to those instincts. I might not always follow them but at least I gave them a good hearing.

Chapter Three

The next morning, as I pulled up to the mansion, I wondered how Griffin was going to deal with Ramos and Jolena. When he had left my apartment earlier, he had seemed preoccupied, unsure as to what his next step should be. I did not envy him. Walking around the side of the house, I pulled up short when I found Ash leaning against a pillar, looking intently into an empty goat pen.

"Morning, Ash. Where's Buddy?"

Ash looked me over and put a cigarette he had been smoking to his mouth. Unlike most musicians that I dealt with, Ash didn't mind the damage that smoking did to his vocal cords. In fact he thought they gave his voice a raspy quality which improved his music.

"Who's Buddy?" he asked, those piercing blue eyes of his now focusing straight on me.

"The goat," I said. "Vale named the goat, Buddy. You know, after Buddy Rich."

Ash laughed humorlessly. "Everything has to mean something to Vale, doesn't it?" he said.

I didn't say anything. I actually found that to be one of Vale's more endearing qualities. He looked deeper than other people into situations.

"Do you know where he is?" I asked.

Ash shrugged. "Don't know, haven't seen it this morning. I don't really care. We'll be going back on tour again soon. Vale is an idiot for getting something permanent. Our life doesn't need attachments. They just bring us down."

I stood there silently, just looking at him. His opinion wasn't new to me. He was in his twenties and part of a rock band. He was living every guy's dream. I wasn't going to disagree with him.

"I'd better go looking for him," I ventured.

Ash smiled at me. "You do that, Trudie."

I turned around and started walking away, feeling Ash's gaze between my shoulder blades until I got out of sight. The property that this particular mansion sat on was huge. That had been one of the benefits to it. It was owned by the recording company and used by various bands and singers as a retreat where they could write songs and record, while not being hassled by any of the issues that affected normal life. I knew the goat could not have got off the property because there was a large brick wall which surrounded the whole place. Despite most goats' legendary ability to escape, I was hoping an eight foot brick wall was going to be one step too far. I was also hoping it had stayed outside because if Buddy had managed to make it inside, there was going to be a big bill for the band to pay when they finally got their latest album out. Regardless, I had to find the goat. Most of the band would still be in bed, sleeping off whatever excesses they had got involved with last night. If I could get the goat back in its pen before Vale woke up, then as long as there had not been too much damage, it would be like the escape never happened. I had a feeling that I was going to need to start looking to see if there was someone who held the job title of goat whisperer. I had a feeling that it would take a miracle for Buddy and me to overcome our initial feelings for each other.

Half an hour later my patience with this particular goat had reached its end. After thinking about the possible damage it could cause, I had done a quick look through the house. There had been no sign of the goat but there had been signs that the goat had at some stage made it inside. I winced as I mentally added up the costs of this particular escape. Once outside again, I headed towards a small lake that I had seen at the back of the property. I knew eventually that most animals found their way to water so I figured that if anything was going to attract our wandering goat, that would be it.

As my phone rang I grabbed it and held it to my ear.

"Hello," I said shortly.

"Hi, Trudie, it's Crystal. Are you busy right now?"

"No," I said. "I'm looking for a goat."

There was silence. "Is that some kind of rock star euphemism that I don't know?" queried Crystal.

I sighed. "No it isn't. I am looking for a goat, an actual goat that one of the band has decided would make for an awesome pet. This thing has been here less than twenty-four hours and it has cut a path of destruction through this house that even these guys would be struggling to replicate. It got out of its yard and now I'm having to look for it on the grounds." I stopped talking for a moment. "Are you laughing at me, Crystal? Because if you're laughing at me I'm hanging up."

"No," Crystal choked out. "I am not laughing at you at all."

She was laughing at me. To be fair, if I called her and she was hunting for a goat, I'd be laughing too.

"What do you want, Crystal?" I asked, choosing at this point to ignore the fact that I was once again the subject of hilarity amongst my friends.

"I need your help," said Crystal.

"Why?" I asked, half paying attention while I was scanning for my lost goat.

"My mother is getting married again."

There was silence as I digested this information. Crystal's mother was a former Las Vegas showgirl who had married Crystal's father long enough to guarantee herself a healthy payday in the form of a child support check.

"How exactly does this affect anyone other than your mother and her soon to be ex-husband?" I asked.

Admittedly that statement had been a little harsh. In my defense, from what I understood this was going to be the woman's eleventh marriage. Of course, that number was fluid as there was some suspicion that Crystal may have missed some of her stepfathers at the point where she simply lost the will to care.

"Roxy has decided she wants me to be involved in this wedding."

"Why?" I asked bluntly. "Have you ever been at any of her other weddings?"

"No," Crystal said. "Most of the men Roxy marries have a distinct allergy to children or even the mention of children so she has always been very careful to keep me away from them."

Like I seemed to do every time I spoke to Crystal about her mother, I thanked whatever forces in the universe that had conspired to give me my mother.

"Roxy's coming to see me to organize details. She wants me to be central to this extravaganza which is going to be held here in LA. I have not told her yet that I am married so that is going to add an entirely new level of pain to this situation, because of course, it is all about her."

I could tell Crystal was starting to get annoyed at the situation her mother had put her into.

"Whatever you need me to do, I'll do," I said.

"Thanks."

I couldn't quite tell if Crystal was grateful that I had agreed to help or irritated that she had to ask for my help. As I came up to the lake I almost dropped to my knees in gratitude.

"I've found my goat," I yelled out excitedly.

"Still not a euphemism?" asked Crystal.

"No," I said. "I'll talk to you when I get home and you can fill me in on what this whole situation is about."

I turned off the phone and slowed down my approach.

"Okay, Buddy," I said soothingly. "Now, I know you've had a bit of excitement today and from the way you're drinking that water I'm sure you've had plenty of exercise. Why don't we go back to the pen and I will personally get you something to eat that you are going to find delicious."

I held out a hand as I tentatively walked up to the goat. He fixed me with a baleful stare and started bleating at me.

I stopped and glared back at him. "What do you want from me, Buddy? I wish you were currently on a farm, running around wherever you wanted but unfortunately that hasn't happened. What you need to do is recognize the circumstances you are in, suck it up and deal as best you can. That's what the rest of us have to do all the time."

He kept bleating. Obviously the tough love speech was not going to work. I raked my hand through my hair in frustration. There was no way I was going to be able to get this goat back to the pen without its direct cooperation. I put my hands on my hips and looked out across the lake. Now that I wasn't focused on the goat, I realized that there was a pile of fabric floating in the middle of the lake. My heart clenched as a sudden thought hit me. Throwing my phone to the ground I pulled off my shoes and ran into the water. When the water got too deep I started swimming. When I got to the middle of the lake my hand reached the fabric. I grabbed for it and felt an arm. I pulled the fabric back to find a body, face down in the lake. I grabbed hold of the person and, using skills learned in childhood swimming lessons, I towed the body back to the shore. Spluttering, I dragged it up the shoreline and began checking for any signs of life. I started screaming for help, hoping that someone was close enough to hear me. Despite the fact one look told me that it was useless, I started first aid. Sometimes miracles happen, but they usually don't happen without some help.

"Trudie." I looked up when I heard Jorge yelling.

"Over here," I called back, panting from the exertion. I continued with the CPR, hoping for some sign that I wasn't wasting my time.

Jorge came running up to me and dropped to his knees beside me.

"Trudie, stop," he said, holding me back by the shoulders. "She's dead, looks like she has been for a while. You can't help her."

By this time I had tears streaming down my face. "You don't understand, she can't be dead. You don't know who she is."

Jorge looked down again. "Isn't that the woman I had to toss out of Ash's bed the other day?"

I slumped back and nodded. "Her name was Jolena and she was Ramos's girlfriend."

"Oh hell," said Jorge.

I completely agreed with him.

Chapter Four

Sitting on the ground, covered in a blanket and surrounded by Jorge, sympathetic musicians and staff, I was obscured from the arriving police. However, I could make out Griffin when he arrived with a panic stricken look of fear on his face. I scrambled to get up as he raced to the body.

"I'm over here," I yelled.

Griffin stopped, turned in my direction and strode towards me.

"I'm okay, but you need to stop…" I didn't get a chance to finish my sentence as I was crushed against his chest.

Griffin held me and for a moment I was terrified that I wasn't going to be able to breathe.

"They told me a woman was dead. I thought it was you. I thought I'd lost you." He buried his head in my shoulder and I wrapped my arms around him.

"It isn't me, it was never close to being me. You need to calm down," I soothed.

The problem with a man who faces life as coldly and calmly as Griffin did is that when they truly care about someone, they have a tendency to lose it completely when there is a threat to that person.

"You need to stop Ramos," I said, pulling away. "The dead woman is her girlfriend."

That got through to Griffin the way nothing else could.

"Watch her," he growled at Jorge and headed straight for his partner.

I watched Griffin stop Ramos before she reached the body. I saw her flick her eyes in my direction and I saw the moment that Griffin told Ramos that her girlfriend had drowned. She stiffened perceptibly but in no other way did she betray what she was feeling. I admired her that self-control and I had expected it. Griffin walked her over to where the body was now lying and she looked down. In that moment I saw nothing on Ramos's face. She was blank as if she was somewhere else. Jorge put an arm around my shoulder and it was only then that I realized that I had tears rolling down my face again.

"It'll be okay," Jorge said as he pulled me closer and started rubbing my back.

Pressing my face into his chest I shook my head. There was no way that things were going to be okay.

When Griffin walked back over to me he looked as if he had the weight of the world on his shoulders. I could see he was torn. He badly wanted to take me as far away from this situation as possible but he couldn't leave Ramos. I wrapped the blanket further around my shoulders.

"You had better stay with her," I said.

Griffin smiled at me gratefully. "Are you sure? Because if you need me…"

I nodded. "I'll be fine."

"I'll make sure she gets home," interrupted Vale as he stood closely behind me.

I could see the surprise on Jorge's face. It was a measure of how worried Griffin was about Ramos that he didn't even notice how far into my personal space Vale was standing.

"They're going to want to interview you all. I won't be involved."

"I understand," I said. "Take care of Ramos, she's the one who needs help right now."

Griffin nodded sharply, turned around and walked away. He passed two men coming towards our group. I remembered Griffin introducing me to them the day before. The younger of the two was Detective Desmond Pickett. I had spent some of the barbecue yesterday talking to his wife. Dana Pickett had been new, just like me and had seemed as overwhelmed as I had by all the other cop partners who already knew each other. Most of the time she had talked about her new baby girl that she had left for the first time with her mother so she could attend the barbecue. Proving her mother was the best of babysitters for a nervous first time mom, we had been interrupted with a constant stream of photos and messages coming through on her phone. All designed to reassure the nervous mother that her baby was fine. I had liked her.

Her husband had seemed very different. He had not interacted well with the other cops and he had seemed ill at ease. He stood in stark contrast to his partner, Marty Fletchall. Detective Fletchall was an older cop. From what I understood he had just got divorced from his third marriage. He had that older silver fox vibe and had got drunk at the party. He had also seemed to act a little overly friendly with some of his coworker's partners. Nothing that could be deemed inappropriate but it still gave me that uncomfortable feeling. Of course that could be because the industry I worked in was well known for the uncomfortable factor at times. There was always the possibility that I was hypersensitive to that kind of thing.

Fletchall smiled at me as he and Pickett came closer.

"Miss Trudie Eyre," he boomed, a little louder than I thought appropriate at a crime scene. "Your reputation precedes you. I wondered when I would be graced with one of your cases."

I wondered if there was a way to make the man shut up. The band members of Crispy Spider were currently looking at me as if I had contracted the plague.

Pickett looked as if he was used to having to apologize for his partner. "What Detective Fletchall means, Miss Eyre, is that we need to speak to you, and everyone here back at the station."

I nodded. I wasn't going to argue today.

Chapter Five

I shivered in the cold interrogation room. At no point during the proceedings had anyone suggested that I have a shower and change my clothes. Now I was desperately trying to stay warm, my hair poking out in every direction and my damp clothes sticking to me in many uncomfortable ways. At least someone had thought to provide me with a new blanket as my last one had become soaked.

The door opened and Detective Fletchall came through. Grabbing a chair, he sat down. I was surprised that Detective Pickett was not with him.

Fletchall raked me up and down. I fought the urge to sneeze to really finish off the drowned rat look that I was obviously now imitating.

He handed me a coffee. "Here," he said gruffly. "This might help."

And just like that he became my new best friend. I really am a simple creature. I wrapped my hands around the mug and let the warmth seep into me.

"Sorry we have to do this. We'll wrap it up quick and get you home."

I was taken aback. My interviews with Griffin and Ramos had never been this pleasant. They were mostly filled with sarcasm and accusations. I had thought that was normal. At no time had I imagined there was a gentler, kinder way to do an interrogation. I should tell Griffin that, because I had to say, at this moment, I was feeling much more cooperative than I had ever felt before in an interrogation.

"So, are you up to telling me what happened?"

I kept the mug clutched in my hand. "I was looking for

Buddy."

"Who is Buddy?" Fletchall interrupted.

"Oh, Buddy is the goat. He belongs to Vale, the drummer. He got out of his pen and I was hunting him down."

Fletchall smiled. "Never a dull moment."

"No. Well, I found Buddy by the lake. I was trying to get him to come back to the pen with me and I saw fabric in the water. I swam out to see what it was and I found Jolena. I dragged her back to the shore and tried to do CPR on her." I blinked back the tears that were welling in my eyes again.

"Why did you start CPR? Was there any indication that she could be saved?"

I shook my head. "It was probably a stupid waste of time. I just…I didn't want her to be dead so I just started and hoped for the best."

Fletchall nodded sympathetically. "Was there anyone else around that you could see?"

I shook my head again. "There wasn't anyone. I screamed for help and Jorge, the security guy, came running. He was the one who called 911."

"You know you did all you could. From what we've been told so far, she had been dead for a while. Nothing you did would have saved her."

I appreciated what he was trying to do. "Thank you for saying that but it doesn't really make me feel that much better."

"It usually doesn't," said Fletchall. "But you need to hold onto that or for the next few days you are going to constantly be wondering what else you could have done. That isn't going to help you or anyone else."

"Thank you," I said.

Fletchall cleared his throat. "You knew it was Jolena Aaron when you pulled her ashore?"

"Yes. I didn't know her surname, but I met her yesterday at the barbecue," I said.

"How did you meet her?" Fletchall asked, his tone becoming a little less sympathetic as if he was trying to strive for a bit of distance.

"Ramos introduced her to me," I said.

"How were they acting towards each other?" Fletchall asked.

"They seemed happy." I could say that honestly. If I had never seen Jolena Aaron at the mansion I would have never guessed they were anything other than a loving couple.

"Was there any reason why she would be at that property last night?" Fletchall asked, a frown on his face.

I could understand. From an outsider's point of view, this whole situation did not add up at all.

"I don't know why she would have been there last night," I said carefully. "I do know she has been at the mansion previously though."

Fletchall looked up, not quite showing the level of interest that I would have assumed that statement merited.

"What was she doing there?"

I grimaced. I had no loyalty to Jolena but I knew that what I was going to say was going to hurt Ramos. Despite the fact our relationship could best be described as barely civil, I really did not want to hurt her this way.

"Jolena had visited the mansion a few nights ago as a fan."

"Go on."

"She was involved in a threesome with one of the band members which became violent and she was removed from the property."

Fletchall didn't look surprised. "We are aware that there was a previous casual encounter between her and Ash Weston. Is there anything else you can add?"

I shook my head, a little shocked. I had not expected Ash to admit to knowing Jolena. I was used to working in an industry where the first and only reaction was always to lie.

"Is there anything else that you can think of that may help with the investigation?"

I shook my head again. As far as I was concerned, that was pretty much it.

"Anything," Fletchall repeated.

Before I could answer, the door to the interrogation room opened, and Detective Pickett and another man walked in.

"What are you doing?" growled Fletchall, throwing an irritated look at his partner.

"This is Miss Eyre's attorney," Pickett said patiently.

He must have seen my look of confusion. The only attorney I had ever used was Reggie Goodman, Monique's husband. I had never seen this man before in my life.

"The record company has organized representation for yourself as well as the band," Pickett explained.

I was stunned. Never before in my life of dealing with celebrities had one of them made the effort to provide me with a lawyer. It almost made me feel like a valued member of a team. I still wasn't sure which team this lawyer was from. But still, I was part of a team which didn't make sure the important people were okay and then forgot about me. That made me feel special.

"Miss Eyre, my name is Harold O'Brien. I need your consent to act as your attorney."

I waited a second before nodding. Despite the fact that as far as interrogations went, this one had been better than any of my previous ones, I was tired, cold and wet. The sooner I was out of here the happier I was going to be.

Fletchall's features tightened.

"I really don't know anything else," I said, hoping to lighten the blow.

I could see I was wasting my breath. Fortunately for me, it seemed Fletchall was saving his ire for his partner.

"Miss Eyre," my new lawyer said, indicating that I should follow him.

I walked past Fletchall and Pickett as they glared at

each other.

"I think there's trouble in paradise," said O'Brien when we were safely out of earshot.

I giggled, releasing some of the pent up emotion that I had been holding onto through the day. "I think you're right."

Following my lawyer, I had another shock. The band was waiting for me. It seemed that the day was full of surprises. Ash, of course, looked completely bored with the entire situation. Personally I thought that was a brave move considering I was sure that he was the one who had known Jolena the best, even if it had been for only a short time. Vale smiled at me encouragingly. The other three members of the band had also waited for me. Dion, Sewell and Tim played guitar, bass and keyboard respectively. I don't think I was emphasizing enough how truly touched I was that the guys had waited for me. I had never had any clients do that for me before and I was at this point willing to forgive every chauvinistic, stupid statement any of these guys had made.

"She's here now, can we go?"

Except for Ash. Obviously the other guys had used peer pressure, or whatever leverage required, to keep him here. Still, I was going to look on the positive side and, for me, support from four out of the five was an amazing result.

I smiled at them. "Thanks for waiting for me."

"Didn't really have a choice."

Once again, I was going to ignore Ash.

"You okay?" Vale asked quietly.

"She's fine," said Ash impatiently as he pushed himself away from the wall he had been leaning against. "I don't know why you need to baby her. She's more capable than the entire lot of us put together." With that he stalked out towards the front of the station, leaving the rest of us looking on in shock. It wasn't often that Ash complimented anyone and regardless of how it was delivered, that was a compliment.

The lawyer, obviously used to dealing with people in the music industry, was the first to recover and cleared his throat. "I am sure I don't need to remind any of you to contact me if there are any further issues with the police. And can you gentlemen just tone it down for a bit. I've got a full schedule for the next few days and the last thing I need is you guys getting involved in a media circus. At the moment we have managed to keep this quiet but you know better than anyone that this is going to blow up in no time at all. When that happens do not be tempted to leave the grounds of the mansion without a security detail, or without letting people know where you are going. Do not comment to anyone and do not do anything stupid."

The guys gave him their best innocent looks but, as I had thought, Harold O'Brien had obviously been working in this industry for a while.

"Just keep your heads down," he warned.

Chapter Six

When we got to the front of the station I was not surprised when I found Lee, Griffin's father, laughing with some of the older cops.

"So strange to see you here, Lee," I said.

Lee smiled, walked over and put an arm around me.

"This is my girl," he stated proudly, and a part of me melted.

I adored Lee. He had been a single father who raised Griffin after his mother had deserted them when Griffin was a baby. He had been a cop who was suddenly thrust into a role he wasn't prepared for. He'd muddled through and Griffin had grown up into the man he was today. Not perfect by any measure but he was a good and strong man and, in my opinion, that meant that Lee had done an amazing job.

"I'm here to take you home," he said, giving Vale a back off look.

I had wondered how long it was going to take Griffin before he realized that he had left me in the care of a man that he didn't know. Jorge looked relieved by this turn of events as well. I loved the men in my life but I had a feeling that I was going to need to have a little talk to them about backing off at times. That kind of protectiveness has a tendency to become smothering. At this moment though, I was cold, wet and wanted to find my way to the nearest shower so I wasn't really in the mood to start an argument.

"Is this your father?" asked Vale, looking nervously at Lee.

Lee beamed.

"Acts like it, doesn't he?" I said. "He's my boyfriend's father."

"The cop," Vale said.

I nodded.

"Ready to go?" asked Lee.

I sneezed in reply and pulled the blanket around me again.

"I think that means yes," Lee smiled at me.

We'll see you tomorrow?" Vale queried.

I nodded as Lee hustled me out of the station.

Once bundled up in the car I could feel Lee's eyes on me.

"You know I would feel much safer if you were watching where you were going," I said tightly.

"You need a new job," Lee said, thankfully returning his eyes to the road.

"I don't need a new job," I said tiredly.

"You definitely need a new job. The odds of you not getting hurt are very quickly running out. Do you have any idea what it would do to Jake if anything happened to you?"

I did know what it would do to Griffin. I also knew that, in his own way, Lee was trying to protect not just his son, but me too. I put a hand on his arm.

"I'm okay," I said softly."

"Today you're okay," Lee said calmly. "I am just a bit concerned about what will happen tomorrow. You're a disaster magnet, Trudie. One of these days your luck is going to run out."

I sat there silently. There wasn't really much I could say. I never went looking for these situations. They just seemed to find me.

Once Lee had dropped me off I stood in my shower and let the hot water wash away the chill that had entered me. It wasn't so much the sight of Jolena's body that bothered me. I'd grown up on a farm so I had been introduced to the concept of death and the cycle of life when I had been young. What bothered me was knowing the devastation that Ramos would be going through. Not only would she be dealing with the death of her girlfriend but she would also be facing the truth about Jolena's infidelity and that was going to hurt her badly.

After my shower I started writing an email to Monique, trying to explain the situation that I had found myself in, but I just kept staring at a blank screen. Throwing random words on the screen didn't help me either. I was becoming so frustrated with my inability to craft even the most basic of messages that I was grateful to hear a knock on my door.

I opened it to find Crystal standing there.

"I need you and Griffin to come to dinner tonight," she said as she walked past me.

"Why?" I closed the door and followed her as she walked into my kitchen and started making herself a coffee.

"My mother is coming over for dinner. I need you there to keep me from doing anything drastic and I need Griffin there to provide some distracting eye candy to keep her attention divided so she doesn't come on to Edwin."

"I don't think we can make it tonight," I said slowly, interested to see how upset Crystal was and the way she was taking it out on my coffee machine. I nudged her aside and took over the coffee making duties while I still had a working coffee maker.

"Why not?" Crystal demanded.

"There has been an incident at work," I said, refusing to look at her.

"Please tell me you didn't find a body."

I smiled at her weakly. "I really wish I could."

Crystal threw her hands in the air. "I spoke to you only a few hours ago and you were looking for a goat. How do we get from looking for a goat to finding a dead body?"

I passed her a coffee. "I found the goat at the lake and the body was in the lake."

"Drowned?" Crystal asked.

I shrugged my shoulders. "I don't know. I saw the

body, went to pull it out and she was dead."

"Could it have been an accident?" Crystal asked.

"It could have been, I guess."

"So, Griffin's working the case?"

I shook my head. "No, not this time. There are some new detectives working this one. The woman was Ramos's girlfriend. Griffin is with her, trying to help."

"Oh no," Crystal gasped. "What was Ramos's girlfriend doing at that place?"

"She'd been there before."

I busied myself with my own coffee. Crystal worked for her father who was one of the biggest casting agents in Hollywood. She knew the excesses of the industry intimately and it didn't take her long to mentally sift through all the possible reasons that Ramos's girlfriend would be at the headquarters for Crispy Spider.

"Groupie?" she queried.

"Unfortunately, yes."

"Did Ramos know she was there?" asked Crystal, quickly recovering from what I had thought was a traumatic revelation.

I shook my head.

"Did you know she was Ramos's girlfriend?"

"I found out yesterday. Griffin and I were still trying to work out how to tell Ramos when I found the body.

"What are you going to do about it?" asked Crystal.

I shrugged. "There is nothing I can do about it. The case is being investigated by a couple of detectives in the Homicide squad. I've been questioned and that is the extent of my involvement in this situation."

"Good," Crystal said firmly.

"What do you mean 'good'?" I asked.

"I mean that you need to keep away from this case as much as possible."

"I've got to go back to work tomorrow," I said ruefully. "My options regarding distance are really not available to me."

"Then at least try being careful this time."

I stifled a frustrated sigh. Despite my reputation, I was always careful. The people around me seemed to have this idea that I went charging heedlessly into dangerous situations. That was so far from the truth as to be laughable. I was one of the most cautious people that I knew. I always weighed up every option, evaluated all risks, before going forward with anything. I was the ultimate planner. Unfortunately, life has a way of spitting on plans and I had learned to be adaptable. I didn't get into these situations because I wanted to get into them. I got into them because Fate had a very sick sense of humor and I seemed to be the whipping boy of the moment.

Crystal eyed me suspiciously.

"So, do you know why your mother is coming to visit?" I asked, desperate to change the topic before Crystal decided to try to institute a curfew policy when it came to me.

Crystal took what was obviously a fortifying sip of her coffee. "Money probably. I only hear from her when she's run out of husbands or money."

"Why do you keep paying her off?"

I was confused by the exceedingly dysfunctional nature of Crystal's relationship with her mother. Roxy would blow into town, drive Crystal crazy until she got some money and then she would wander to another part of the world and start torturing someone else.

"I pay her off because it means she leaves. If I don't give her money, she stays in my life and I really don't want that to be an option."

I sipped my own cup of coffee thoughtfully. "You know it might be worth refusing to pay her anything. Once she realizes that you are no longer an easy mark she might leave you alone."

Crystal sighed. "I have tried that before, but it comes down to a battle of wills. Who can last longer? Generally I find that I cave because I just want her away from me."

"And yet she keeps coming back. Whenever she turns up you go through this crazy time and it can't be healthy for you. Maybe it has reached the point where you have to make a stand. You know, short term pain for long term gain."

"I know, I know. But it wouldn't just be pain. I would have to wait her out and that woman can be annoying. She turns up everywhere I am and she has no problem with humiliating me whenever she can." Crystal dropped her voice. "I want to minimize the time she spends with Edwin. She'll want to sabotage our relationship. I know she will. She'll see him as a drain on the money that she feels should rightfully go to her. I will do anything to protect him from that."

"Edwin knows about your mother. Nothing she says is going to have any impact on how he feels about you," I said gently.

It was true. Edwin worshiped the ground that Crystal walked on. It would take more than the words of one money hungry mother to change that.

"I tried to get him to leave while my mom was here," Crystal said.

I snorted. That was going to work. I could not see any circumstance where Edwin would willingly leave Crystal's side when her mother was in town.

"That was pretty much his reaction as well," Crystal murmured.

"So what are you going to do?" I asked.

Crystal shrugged. "Just try to get through the next few days. You're right though, I need to stop giving in to the woman. If I don't this is going to happen for the rest of my life because I just know she's going to outlast me. She'll probably end up fighting Edwin and any kids I might have over the will."

I grimaced. That was a cheery thought.

Crystal took a swallow of her coffee and put the cup down with a decisive thud.

"I can do this," she muttered, more to convince herself than to convince me. "Thanks for listening, Trudie. Keep out of trouble this time."

I loved how everyone thought I could prevent myself from being in these situations. If there was a way for me to avoid finding a dead body, I would be the first to attempt it.

Chapter Seven

Once again I found myself staring at a blank screen, trying to find the best way to tell my boss that, despite my best efforts, I had found myself in a police interrogation room again. There was a nagging part of me that kept wondering whether this was going to be the moment that Monique decided that I wasn't worth the trouble. After much deliberation I decided that the blunt approach was probably best. I outlined the situation in bald terms and almost cringed as I pressed the Send button. I barely had time to turn off my computer when my phone rang.

"Hello," I said timidly.

"You contemplated not answering the phone didn't you?" Monique asked dryly.

"Of course not." I couldn't help the fact that I was nodding my head.

"I know you're nodding."

Some days I hated the fact that Monique knew me so well.

"Do you need Reggie?" she asked.

"No," I replied. "The recording company organized a lawyer for me. He got me out of the station."

"Really?"

I could understand the incredulity in Monique's voice. I was still in a state of shock over the fact that I hadn't been left behind and forgotten.

"I think it might be better to pull you from this job."

It took me a second to process what Monique was saying. "Why would you do that?"

"I don't want to risk you getting hurt."

"Jorge's there too," I reminded her. "Are you planning

on pulling him from the job as well?"

"Jorge doesn't suffer from the same run of bad luck that you seem to have."

I loved the fact that Monique seemed to be blaming my luck and not me. Hopefully that meant that my job was still safe.

"Maybe we should look at increasing security on this assignment," Monique mused.

"If you can find somebody," I grimaced.

According to Jorge, none of the other security staff would willingly work with me. My reputation had, in my opinion, been blown completely out of proportion at the agency and Jorge was the only person who could be convinced to take an assignment with me. Usually it didn't bother me. Frankly, I preferred to work with Jorge. Unfortunately, I knew that it made things difficult for Monique when she needed to find more than one staff member to work with me. The rumor mill would go into overdrive and all of a sudden phone calls from Monique would start to go unanswered.

"Maybe I'll get lucky and one of the new hires will not have heard about you yet."

It was good to see that Monique's positive spin on the situation was hoping that my reputation was not included in the welcome pack for new employees.

"Regardless, I have been notified by the band's management that they do not want you at work tomorrow."

"I've been fired?" That didn't seem fair.

"Of course not. The band and their management are going to be in crisis meetings all day tomorrow and they don't need you or Jorge. Naturally, they put it a different way, something about being sensitive to the stressful situation you faced today and that you deserved a day off."

I nodded. Translated that meant that from a public relations point of view, the next couple of days were going to be challenging and they just wanted to make sure the band was prepared to face it. They didn't want outsiders interfering with their risk management program. Despite the warm and fuzzy moment at the station, Jorge and I were definitely still considered outside guns for hire with no real loyalty to the band. However the band and its management decided to play things, we were not going to be part of the decision making process. I was perfectly fine with that.

"You'll be required back at the mansion the next day though. Hopefully I'll be able to get someone extra for security then."

"Good luck with that." I wasn't holding my breath.

"Promise me that you will not take any risks." Monique's voice sounded serious.

That made me feel bad. Monique had always supported me and the strain in her voice was telling me that I was causing her some concern.

"I promise," I said quietly.

After saying goodbye to Monique I sat heavily on the couch and my head dropped into my hands. I knew that the people who cared about me were getting worried. The sheer terror I had seen on Griffin's face at the mansion was a clear indicator that each of them was having nightmares that the next time I wasn't going to be just a traumatized bystander. I wiped my hands over my face. Maybe I should talk to Monique about finding a quiet job for my next assignment. Maybe she had some filing she needed done. How much trouble could I get into with that?

I jumped at the sound of my phone ringing again. Thinking it might be Griffin, I answered it without checking.

"Trudie, it's Vale."

I felt my forehead crease. "Hi, Vale. Is there something I can help you with?"

Vale cleared his throat nervously. "I just wanted to make sure you were okay, after what happened today."

"I'm fine," I said automatically. I really wasn't fine but I couldn't say that to my client. At all times I had to at least give the impression that I had everything under control, even if I didn't.

"Heard you weren't going to be in tomorrow. I was just wondering if you were coming back at all or whether you were going to abandon us? Buddy wanted to know. He's really quite fond of you."

I laughed. "Now I know you're lying. That goat hates me with a passion."

Vale chuckled. "I think hate is a bit of a strong word."

"I don't think it's strong enough for the way that goat feels about me."

There was silence as we both seemed to be searching for something else to say.

"I'll be back the day after tomorrow. Tell Buddy I'll see him then," I said.

"I'll do that," Vale replied. "Take care of yourself."

I ended the call and stared at my phone for a few moments. I hadn't been expecting to be contacted by any of the band directly. I had become quite fond of all of them over the last month, except Ash of course. That in itself was unusual. Generally, after a month working for any of my clients, I was wondering how much more I could take. In some cases I would be actively looking for the nearest escape route. This job had been relatively pleasant, if I didn't take into account the hedonistic rock and roll lifestyle which, surprisingly, I seemed to be able to ignore. Still, I hadn't expected any of them to care. It was nice.

I yawned widely, surprised by how tired I was. I curled up on the couch and fell asleep, hoping my dreams would be untouched by the events of the day. I came awake suddenly as I felt myself being lifted up. I opened my eyes to see Griffin looking down at me with that same worried expression that seemed to be on his face far too often.

"You're home."

He kissed me on the forehead. "Yes, sweetheart. Go back to sleep, I just figured you'd be more comfortable in bed."

"Thank you," I said as he laid me down on the mattress.

I waited for him while he was in the bathroom getting ready for bed. When he stretched out beside me I turned to him and felt safer as his arms wrapped around me.

"How is Ramos doing?"

Griffin took in a deep breath. "She's holding it together. I had to tell her about Jolena cheating on her. I didn't want her getting blindsided by Fletchall with that little piece of information."

"Did she have any idea?"

Griffin shook his head. "Seems Jolena had issues in the past but Ramos thought that they had worked through them. From what I could tell, Ramos didn't know Jolena was cheating but she wasn't completely shocked."

"How did she know her?"

"Jolena's a model. Not an overly famous one or anything. Seems she did a bit on the side, enough to keep her going but not enough to hit the big time. She was also starting to do some acting work, small bits really. Ramos met her in some coffee shop they both go to and they hit it off. It seems they went from there. Ramos thought it was exclusive but from what I've been hearing, Jolena was a bit of a wild one. She liked moving in certain circles. Partying with musicians would be right up her alley."

"I hope she'll be okay," I said quietly against his chest.

"She's strong," Griffin murmured. "She's got a lot of family around her and they're helping."

"Good."

"I got a scare today, sweetheart."

"I'm sorry." I held onto him a little tighter.

"We got a call about a female body at that property and I knew that you were the only woman they have working there at the moment. I honestly thought I'd lost you. I never want to feel that way again. I never want to go through what Ramos is going through right now."

I knew I couldn't say anything that was going to make this better.

"I know you don't do anything to cause this. I know it's just my fears but I wish I could find a way to wrap you up and keep you safe."

"Monique is worried too. She is looking at putting on a second security person until they find out what happened."

"Good. I know Jorge keeps an eye on you but I wouldn't mind somebody else there to watch your back as well."

I felt a light kiss on the top of my head. "Just stay safe for me, sweetheart."

I nodded and felt myself drifting off, secure in his arms.

Chapter Eight

"Wake up, sweetheart. You need to get ready for work."

I opened my eyes slowly and found Griffin, fully dressed, with his hand on my shoulder.

"Not going to work today. Monique told me they didn't want me."

I turned over and pulled the covers over my head. Griffin pulled them away and I grumbled in his general direction.

"What's going on? Have you been fired?"

I really didn't appreciate the hopeful quality in his voice.

"No, I haven't been fired. I'm just not going to work today. The band is in crisis talks with their management over what happened with Jolena. My input is not considered necessary in those circumstances."

Griffin's face tightened. "So, they're circling the wagons, are they?"

I nodded. "Probably. Once management, public relations and lawyers get involved, that's what they seem to do."

"And our chances of finding out the truth get more and more unlikely."

Griffin sounded bitter and I didn't blame him. It was bad enough when he was investigating a normal case, let alone one where he had an emotional stake in it.

"Are Detectives Fletchall and Pickett any good?" I asked.

Griffin shrugged. "I don't know Pickett at all. He's new to the precinct. Fletchall has been there forever and he's a pretty good detective. Doesn't always get along with everybody but then who really does?"

I sat up in bed and rubbed a hand over my face.

"Have they told you anything about Jolena yet? Do they know what happened?"

Griffin smiled ruefully. "They're not going to tell me a thing about this case. The victim being Ramos's girlfriend means that the two of us are now kept on a strictly need to know basis. I'll probably be spoken to at some point but they are going to keep me as far away from this case as it is possible to get."

"Enjoy the interrogation. I have to say that the one I had yesterday was the most pleasant that I ever had."

Griffin quirked an eyebrow. "Really?"

I nodded enthusiastically. "Detective Fletchall brought me coffee and he was nice to me. You might want to take notes."

"Are you complaining about my technique?"

"When it comes to the interrogation room, yes I am."

Griffin smiled and brushed his lips over mine. "I'll see you when I get home."

I smiled back at him. "See you then."

When I heard the door close I fell back onto the bed, pulled the covers over my head and closed my eyes.

I heard a key in the door.

"Did you forget something?" I called out, although it was slightly muffled by the covers.

I didn't hear a reply and I turned my head slightly.

"Griffin?"

I screamed when a figure jumped on top of me.

"Don't panic, it's just me."

I ripped the covers down. "Crystal, what the hell are you doing? You almost gave me a heart attack."

Crystal smiled unrepentantly.

"Okay, that does it. I want my emergency key back now." I glared at her.

Crystal sat up on the bed.

"Fine, here it is," she said, dropping the key on my

bedside table.

I could feel my eyes narrowing. That had been too easy.

"You've made a copy, haven't you?"

"Several," Crystal grinned.

I dropped my head back on the pillow. "You've got to stop doing that," I growled. "Griffin's pretty much living here these days. He's generally armed and when it comes to my protection he's on a bit of a hair trigger. You come into this apartment when he's not expecting it and I can't be held accountable for what happens next."

Crystal dismissed my worries with a wave of her hand. "I have complete faith in Griffin's reflexes. Anyway, how else am I going to be able to get an eyeful of him as he walks out of the shower?"

I shook my head. Crystal is deliriously happily married to my friend, Edwin. Despite that inescapable fact, she has got the strangest bucket list which includes getting a glimpse of Griffin when he walks out of the shower. Edwin can't really say much because his bucket list includes watching me utilize skills that I had learned at a previous job at a strip club. I hadn't thought my pitiful attempts at using a stripping pole for fitness would interest anyone, not even my boyfriend. But Edwin was insistent that he and Crystal should get a show. I think it had more to do with the comedic value of seeing the lack of coordination that I bring to dancing, and elevating it to swinging around a pole. I was beginning to think that our friendship had wandered into a weird territory.

"I knew Griffin was gone. I watched him leave," Crystal said airily.

"Because that doesn't sound creepy at all," I said. "Now that we've established that we really need to discuss our relationship boundaries, what are you doing here?"

"My mom came to dinner last night."

Oh, right. I'd forgotten about that.

"Let me get up and I'll make you a cup of coffee."

"And pancakes?" Crystal asked hopefully.

"And pancakes," I agreed, wondering how a break-in had ended up with me catering for the perpetrator. "Just let me get dressed first."

I struggled to get out from underneath the covers and landed awkwardly on the floor. Crystal looked at me appraisingly.

"That's what you wear to bed?" she queried.

I looked down at myself. My pajamas looked fine to me and, more importantly, they were comfortable.

"Yes, what's wrong with them?"

"Nothing," Crystal said hurriedly. "I'm just now beginning to appreciate that love is truly blind and how much Griffin must really love you."

"I'd be a lot nicer to me if you want those pancakes," I grumbled.

"If you add some ice cream to them I'll say whatever you want," Crystal called out after me.

In no time at all I was scooping ice cream onto Crystal's pancakes.

"So," I said with some trepidation, "how did last night go?"

"She didn't even try to come on to Edwin," Crystal said morosely.

I paused with the spoon going to my mouth. "Isn't that a good thing?"

"Yes, but it isn't the way we do things. My mom comes into town, tries to seduce any guy I'm with, destroys my life, gets her money, and then leaves. She does not try to be nice and then announce she is marrying her soul mate who is a plumber."

"What's wrong with a plumber?" I asked, curious to see her answer.

"There is nothing wrong with a plumber but my mother does not marry plumbers. She marries investment bankers, mob guys, rich men. She does not marry a plumber. She does not ask me to be her bridesmaid at the wedding and she does not tell me that she loves me."

"So, you're upset because your mother is acting like a mother," I said slowly.

I understood where she was coming from. After all I had heard about Crystal's mother, these actions were not what I was expecting.

"Exactly," said Crystal.

"Wait a minute," I said. "She said she loved you?"

Crystal nodded. "Well, it was more of a 'love ya, babe,' at the end of the night so I'm not entirely sure about the feeling behind it but the words were definitely there."

"Is she dying?"

"That was my first thought as well," Crystal exclaimed. "Edwin said I was just being morbid."

"Religious conversion?"

"My mom getting religion?" Crystal chewed her pancakes thoughtfully. "I don't really see that happening."

"Then what do you think it is?"

Crystal shrugged. "I don't know and it's that not knowing that is freaking me out. I keep thinking that the other shoe is going to drop and I'm worried that I'll be taken by surprise. I don't deal well with being taken by surprise, Trudie."

"So, what are you going to do?" I asked.

"I want you to come with me when we go dress shopping."

Not what I was expecting but I could be flexible.

"When did you want to go?"

Crystal looked at her watch. "Pretty much now."

"Now?" I asked.

"The wedding is in two days," Crystal said as she shoveled the last of the pancakes into her mouth.

"Two days?"

"Why do you keep repeating everything I'm saying? The wedding is in two days. I'm a bridesmaid and I need a dress. My mom is waiting for me to go shopping with her this morning. I figured that since you haven't left for work already that you've probably got the day off."

I was impressed with her deductive reasoning.

"I need you to act as a human shield if this gets too weird with my mom."

"Exactly how am I supposed to act as a human shield?"

"I don't know. Do whatever it is you do at work. For goodness sake, you work with high maintenance people all the time. Do what you do there. Distract, deflect, stop me from killing her."

It was good to know my skills had practical applications that could be used in my personal life as well as my professional one.

Chapter Nine

Despite the many stories that Crystal had told me about her mother, I had never had the pleasure of meeting the woman. Due to my loyalty to Crystal though, I had already prejudged her and my opinion wasn't pretty. As we waited outside the dress store I noticed that Crystal was moving constantly.

"What are you doing?" I asked.

"I don't know," she said. "I'm nervous about the fact that I'm looking for a dress with my mother. How messed up is that?"

It was messed up, made even more so by the fact that Crystal is one of the most confident people that I know. I disliked Crystal's mother a little bit more in that moment, knowing that her presence was causing my friend's anxiety.

I put my hand over hers. "You need me to do anything, just tell me. If you need to get out of here I can fake a medical emergency in a heartbeat."

Crystal laughed. "No you can't. You're a worse actor than Edwin."

That was harsh. Accurate, but harsh.

"How much acting does it take to fall down in a faint? I could do that. You could tell your mom that I've got some weird tropical Australian disease. She'll believe it."

"Thank you," Crystal said as she gave me a hug. "I'm glad you're here."

I hugged her back. "So am I."

"Liar."

Okay, fine. I was lying. I couldn't think of many things worse than shopping for a bridesmaid dress for a wedding for Crystal's mom. If there was a potential for a bridezilla moment, this was it.

"There she is."

I turned around to look in the direction that Crystal was indicating.

Crystal's mom didn't exactly look like I had pictured her. Admittedly, any time I had imagined Crystal's mother, the words Las Vegas showgirl had featured prominently, so I had always pictured her in costume. That may have been a little inappropriate for the streets of Los Angeles. She was dressed pretty conservatively in a simple skirt and top, something you would expect with any bride-to-be. Her blonde hair was perfectly styled and she walked in that confident way that some women have. Those women that know that eyes are turning in their direction wherever they are going. She was taller than I expected. Crystal was tiny. Without high heels she barely reached five feet. Crystal's coloring was in marked contrast to her mother. I'd never really thought before about how much more Crystal looked like her father than her mother. She stopped in front of us and awkwardly went to kiss Crystal on the cheek.

"Roxy, this is my friend, Trudie, the one I told you about. Trudie, this is my mother, Roxy."

I put my hand out, for no other reason than to avoid the whole awkward social kissing scene.

Roxy grasped my hand. "It's so good to meet you, Trudie. Crystal has told me so much about you. I feel like I know you already."

I smiled hesitantly. No way was I going to bring up how well I knew her based on what Crystal had told me. That was never going to be a conversation that ended well.

Crystal glanced between the two of us. "Should we go inside and get started?" she queried.

Roxy smiled. "That would be a great idea."

I was surprised to find that the shop we had come to wasn't as exclusive as I would have expected Crystal's mother to have chosen. Maybe things were different this time round.

Crystal turned to her mother. "What did you want me

to wear?"

Roxy smiled. "Just pick something out that you think you would like. We're not really going with a theme for the wedding. We just want everyone to be happy and comfortable."

Crystal turned around but not before I noticed her raised eyebrows. I had a feeling that this new version of her mother was causing her to question everything she knew about the woman. After browsing through the racks Crystal entered the fitting rooms with her arms filled with dresses. I kept wandering through the store, not purposely avoiding Roxy, but just keeping my distance. I was admiring a deep blue dress in a soft fabric when Roxy came up behind me.

"You don't like me very much, do you?"

In this moment, I had a choice. I could go with the socially acceptable fantasy version of my opinion, or I could go with the truth.

"Not really."

You would think that after all the time I worked in Hollywood I would have made a different choice.

Roxy looked surprised. "I wasn't expecting you to say that."

I hadn't been expecting it either. "Crystal is a good friend and I adore her. You being here causes problems and I'm naturally wired to solve problems. I'm not sure how to fix this for her."

Roxy nodded. "I understand. I haven't been the best of mothers. I know that."

I stayed silent. There was no way I was going to contradict her self-assessment now.

"The way John is with his family has made me have a good hard look at myself. I haven't been too impressed with what I've seen."

I quietly listened to her as I put the dress back on the rack.

"I want to do better with Crystal. I have made so many

wrong decisions in my life and most of them centered around her. I want a way to fix what I've done."

"Maybe telling her that, rather than me, would be a good start," I said.

Roxy smiled ruefully. "You'd think so but I seem to have trouble saying those words to Crystal. You seem to be easier to talk to."

I shook my head. "No, it's just that you don't care whether I like you or not. It seems that despite the way you've treated Crystal all her life, you've started to care."

"I don't know how to reach her. Maybe too much has happened for us to ever work things out between us."

Roxy looked distressed by that thought. That more than anything else gave me hope that she really meant what she was saying.

"How about laying it out there for her. After everything that's happened between you I don't think that anything less than complete honesty is going to work."

Roxy nodded. "I want her to meet John. Maybe when she sees him, sees the kind of man he is, maybe then she'll realize that I'm not the same person I was."

"That could be a good idea," I said.

"Trudie, I want to say something to you but I don't want to hurt your feelings." Roxy looked nervous.

That was sweet. I could have told her that, considering the industry I worked in, she was going to need to come up with something pretty spectacular to actually manage to hurt my feelings.

"I want you to go away."

I stopped and stared. Although not particularly insulting to me, it was actually something I'd heard many times before, I was a little perplexed.

"I think I need to spend some time alone with Crystal and I think you being here is going to stop it being as honest as it needs to be."

That was pretty blunt.

"I'll just check with Crystal and see if she's okay with

that," I said.

I poked my head into the fitting room. "You decent?"

"Rarely," Crystal called out. "Come in anyway, I could do with some help with this dress."

I squeezed into the fitting room with her. "What's the problem?"

"I can't quite get this zip to come all the way up."

I looked down at the dress. I had a feeling it wasn't going to fit well. Crystal has curves and some of the clothes that were in these stores were not forgiving of even the smallest hint of an hourglass figure.

"Never mind, I can see from the look on your face that this one isn't going to work. Can you just get the zip down for me?"

I started pulling it down. "As long as you never mention a word of this to Edwin."

Crystal smiled. "I promise." She turned around and faced me.

"I've got to go."

Crystal's face fell. "Work call you in?"

I shook my head. "No, your mom wants me to leave."

"Excuse me."

I could see Crystal wasn't reacting well to that statement.

"Your mom wants to spend a day with you. She's trying to connect with you, Crystal. I know you brought me here to act as interference but I really think you should at least hear the woman out. If I'm here it kind of wrecks the mood."

"And what if this is simply more of the same garbage that she's been peddling to me my entire life. People don't change."

"Sometimes they do, Crystal, if they are motivated enough. I'm not saying you have to believe her. I'm not even saying that you have to have anything more to do with her after today. All I'm suggesting is that you listen to what she has to say. Give her today, and tomorrow morning make a decision as to whether you still want her in your life. Even if today is a massive disaster and you end up never wanting to see her again, how is that any different from the way you felt yesterday morning? You are not going to lose anything. You'll still have your dad, you'll still have Edwin and you'll still have me. Hell, I'll even throw in Griffin if it'll make you happy."

"Oh, because that's just a dream come true," Crystal said sarcastically.

"We're in a highly emotional moment so I'm going to ignore that comment about the love of my life," I said wryly.

Crystal giggled. "Okay, you're right. You should go. It was probably a bit of a coward move to bring you along."

"I would never say that." I pulled her close to give her a hug.

"You realize we're hugging and I'm half naked," Crystal said.

"We're not telling Edwin about that either."

Chapter Ten

I was surprised to find Ramos waiting at my apartment.

"Liza, are you okay?"

I immediately cursed myself for the stupid question. Of course she wasn't okay.

"I need to talk to you, Trudie."

"Uh, sure, whatever you want." I clumsily unlocked my door. "Come on in." I motioned her into my apartment. "Can I get you a coffee, something to eat?"

"How long did you know?" Ramos asked suddenly.

"Know what?"

"How long did you know that Jolena was cheating on me?"

I clasped my hands together. "I didn't know who she was until we met at the barbecue."

"Why didn't you tell me?"

"What was I going to say?" I hoped she would understand. "I didn't know how to approach the situation and it wasn't the place to say it."

Ramos turned away from me. "I knew there was something wrong with you at the barbecue. You were acting strange, even by your standards." She turned back to me. "I want you to tell me everything that happened."

I really didn't want to do that.

"Are you sure? Maybe you should just leave this to Fletchall and Pickett. I gave them the information. They are the ones who are following it up."

"Everything, Trudie."

I swallowed nervously. "The guys in the band are currently working on a new album so they are pretty much cloistered away during the day. There are a minimal number of staff on site, mostly just to keep things ticking along smoothly. We make sure the guys get what they want so nothing interrupts the creative process. At nights they sometimes have parties. Most of the attendees at these parties are female, a lot of them are models. The stereotype of rock stars hooking up with models is pretty accurate." I grimaced as I belatedly remembered that Jolena had been a model.

"Go on," Ramos waved her hand.

"On those nights when the band is partying, the women compete with each other to spend some time with the guys. There's a hierarchy. As you would expect, the lead singer is at the top of that hierarchy. Ash's tastes sometimes run a little wild. My role at these parties is to make sure things don't get too out of hand. That night Ash had two women with him. I heard some screaming and I followed Jorge into the room. We found Ash sitting back while these two women were fighting each other. Jolena was doing some damage to the other girl. Jorge tried to separate them and found it really tough. Some of the other guys came in to find out what was happening and eventually we got everything calmed down. The other girl was a bit messed up. She had definitely come off second best in the fight. Jolena was told to leave and that she would never be welcomed back. It was the only time I had ever seen her there. When I saw her at the barbecue I didn't know how to react. I am so sorry for what has happened."

We both stood silently and the seconds ticked by at an agonizingly slow pace.

"This is your fault," Ramos accused. "If it hadn't been for you, this would never have happened."

A part of me wanted to defend myself, but the look in Ramos's eyes were those of someone who was not going to listen to reason. Anything that I had to say in my defense was just going to add fuel to the fire.

"You are surrounded by death. It was only a matter of time before we got caught up in it."

I stayed silent, concentrating on the floor in front of

me.

"I know Jolena had her problems but this shouldn't have happened to her."

"I'm sorry," I said quietly.

"That doesn't help me," said Ramos.

"I know."

"They said you tried to save her."

I nodded.

Ramos turned and walked out of my apartment. I let out the breath I hadn't realized I was holding.

I didn't quite know what to do next. I was concerned about Ramos. She was calm, like she always was, but it seemed to be a thin veneer. I wondered where Griffin was. I had thought that he would be with Ramos today.

There was a knock at my door. I opened it, half expecting Ramos to have come back.

"Detective Fletchall, what are you doing here?" I asked, surprised to see the police officer at my front door.

Fletchall smiled. "I was in the neighborhood and had a couple of questions for you if that is okay. If you want to check with your lawyer first I can wait."

I smiled. "No, that's fine. I really don't think I have anything to add to what I've already given you, but if you want to come in, you're welcome."

I stepped back as the detective walked into the apartment.

"Would you like a coffee?"

Fletchall smiled. "That would be great. It's been a bit of a rough day. You can probably imagine."

I could. I had seen the effects on Griffin in the first days after he caught a case. It was a mad scramble for clues before the trail grew cold.

"Grab a seat." I indicated a chair at the dining table and started making a coffee for him

"So what did you need to ask me?"

Fletchall cleared his throat. "The word we are getting from the guys in the band is that Jolena was only at the mansion that one time when she was thrown out. Is that true?"

I nodded. "As far as I know it is. I don't remember seeing her there any other time. We have had quite a few people through at some of these parties but I would have thought that I would notice Jolena. She had something about her that stood out."

Fletchall nodded as I passed him a coffee. "She sure did. Thanks for that." He raised the coffee to take a sip. "That's really good, exactly what I needed. You say that you saw her at the barbecue. Do you think that she recognized you?"

I shrugged. "I don't know. She didn't give any indication that she did. I felt a little uncomfortable about the situation so I went to speak to Dana Pickett, your partner's wife."

"I don't think I met her," Fletchall said as he started writing things in his notebook.

"Well, Dana and I talked for a while and then Griffin and I left."

"Did you tell Griffin about Jolena?"

I nodded. "When we got home that night I told him."

"Do you know if he told Ramos about it?"

"I don't think he told her until after Jolena died. Everything happened so fast that morning, I don't think he got a chance."

I heard the front door to the apartment open. I looked up and was surprised to see Griffin walking into the room. Griffin stopped at the sight of Fletchall and me sitting at the dining table.

"What's happening here?" he growled.

I smiled up at him. "Detective Fletchall just wanted to have a chat about the case," I said.

Griffin did not return my smile, instead glaring at Fletchall.

"How's Ramos?" I asked, more to cut through the tension that seemed to have enter the room along with

Griffin.

"She's getting through it," Griffin replied and then stared at Fletchall meaningfully. "I am sure she is hoping that the case gets solved quickly so that she can start making sense of the whole thing."

Obviously getting the hint, Fletchall stood up. "Thanks for the coffee, Trudie. And for the talk. Griffin's a lucky man. Not many girlfriends would be so understanding of the amount of time he spends with Liza."

I almost groaned. I could see Griffin bristle. The last thing I needed was for Griffin to get in an argument with one of his coworkers. I don't know why cops seemed to always feel the need to score points off each other. I blamed the long hours and the lack of sleep.

Fletchall made his way past Griffin, the cocky grin on his face seemed to be almost daring Griffin to take a swing. When the door closed behind Fletchall, Griffin glowered at me.

"What was he doing here?" he barked.

"Please tell me you are not angry with me because the detective in charge of the case of the body that I found yesterday came to talk to me," I said with a measure of serenity that I didn't necessarily feel.

I watched as Griffin took in a breath and I could see him striving to reach a level of calm that wouldn't provoke either of us to fly off the handle.

"I hardly think that it's appropriate for him to visit you at your home and have a coffee with you."

I could feel my jaw drop. "What are you talking about? You did it all the time when you were investigating cases. I couldn't get rid of you. Everywhere I turned you seemed to be there."

"That was different," Griffin said defensively.

"How was it different?"

"It just was. Anyway, he's supposed to be looking for Jolena's murderer, not chatting you up."

"He was not chatting me up. He just had a couple

more questions for me and he was in the neighborhood. Wait a minute, did you say that Jolena was murdered?" I queried.

Griffin nodded. "Looks like she was strangled before she went into the water."

"Ramos knows?"

Griffin nodded.

"She came here."

"What do you mean she came here?"

"Ramos came to see me."

Griffin sat heavily on the couch. "Why on Earth would she do that?"

"I don't think she's coping as well as we're all expecting her to."

"What did she say?"

"She wanted to know how long I'd known about Jolena cheating. She wanted details."

"Oh hell." Griffin leaned back against the couch and closed his eyes. "Anything else I need to know?"

"No, not really."

Griffin opened his eyes. "What else, Trudie? I know there was something else. You really can't lie worth a damn, can you?"

"It doesn't matter," I said, feeling uncomfortable.

"Sweetheart, tell me."

I sat down next to him and curled into his side. "She blames me for what happened to Jolena. She said that there is death all around me and it was only a matter of time before someone close to me got caught up in it."

"Oh, sweetheart," Griffin said as he put an arm around me. "She's hurting. She got hit with the double whammy. First, Jolena gets killed and then she finds out that she was cheating on her. It's only natural that she's going to lash out at someone. You being the one to find Jolena and the fact you knew about the cheating makes you the most convenient target."

I nodded against his chest.

"Please tell me that you are not taking what she said seriously."

I sighed heavily. "She's right. Everywhere I turn I seem to trip over a body."

Griffin stroked his hand down my arm. "Yeah, but you also help the people who are affected by the death. In most cases you are precisely the right person to deal with the situation. Maybe there's a reason for you being the one to find these bodies."

I looked up and arched an eyebrow at him. "Do you actually believe that or are you just trying to make me feel better?"

Griffin smiled sheepishly. "Maybe a little of both."

I brushed a kiss on his cheek. "Thank you, you are very sweet to me sometimes."

"I'm sweet to you all the time."

I grinned. "Do you still have a copy of that file you made up to have me charged with assault that time I accidentally elbowed you in the eye?"

Griffin nodded.

"Then that means you're only sweet some of the time. That file was supposed to be destroyed."

Griffin laughed. "It's a memento, a fond memory of when we first met."

I pulled away from him and stood up. "If you think that's a fond memory, you have got some serious issues, my friend. Anyway, what are you doing home so early? Didn't you just go to work a few hours ago?"

"I've been suspended," Griffin said abruptly.

I dropped back onto the couch and I'm sure my mouth was wide open.

"What happened?"

"They're investigating Ramos for her girlfriend's murder and I may have told my lieutenant how much of an idiot he was."

"And they suspended you for that?" I asked.

Griffin rolled his eyes. "Okay, I wasn't suspended so

much as told I had to take leave that I had accrued. I'm not to show my face in the precinct until Lieutenant Ellis has taken my photo down from the dart board in the break room."

"Okay," I said slowly. "How long do they think that will be?"

"Not sure. Usually Ramos pulls it down at some point, when she gets annoyed with seeing it up there. But she's suspended as well so it could take a while."

"How often does it end up there?" I asked.

Griffin gave me a sheepish grin, along with his most innocent look. "Pretty regularly."

"You really need to work on being more friendly with people," I sighed, knowing I was fighting a losing battle.

He put an arm around my shoulders. "Why? The people I care about are fine with the way I am. I'm not really bothered by what anyone else says. You put up with me. Why should I care about everybody else?"

"But you're overlooking the fact that I have an amazing ability to accept some of your less endearing qualities," I said. "And even then, there are some days when you stretch even my almost limitless patience."

"And that's what makes you special," Griffin grinned as he stood up.

"What are you doing?" I asked.

"I'm going to call Ramos, see if she needs anything," Griffin said as he pulled out his phone.

"Good idea," I replied.

As he walked away my phone started ringing and I checked the screen.

"Hi, Monique."

"Ma petite, how are you today?"

"I'm fine, Monique. What's the problem?"

"Why do you think there's a problem?"

"Just a feeling."

Monique was quiet for a moment. "I can't get anyone to do security with you."

"Nobody?" I was dumbfounded. "You are telling me that none of your big, strong and, to most other people, dangerous security guys are willing to work with me." Jorge had been only too pleased to enlighten me to the fact that I had an unusual reputation at the agency, but I hadn't expected such a blanket refusal.

"Did they give any reasons?" I asked.

"I got lots of reasons," Monique said waspishly. "I'm just not sure that I believe many of them."

Monique sounded annoyed. That did not bode well. This was a woman who was calm in the face of everything. At worst I had seen her slightly perturbed. I had never known her to be actually annoyed before.

"I believe I may need to do some further recruitment."

A part of me wanted to laugh. "I think the only way that is going to work is if the current security staff aren't allowed to speak to the new recruits. My understanding is that my reputation is pretty well known."

"Don't worry, ma petite. I will find someone who is not afraid of gossip and innuendo. My Reggie has offered to do it if we cannot find anyone else."

That was sweet. Unfortunately Reggie was about half the size of Jorge. Despite the fact the man was lethal in the courtroom, I wasn't sure if he would be quite as effective in the security field.

"I don't want you to worry about it, Monique. I am sure that Jorge and I can handle anything that happens."

"I worry about you, Trudie," Monique said softly.

"I know. Everybody seems to worry about me but I'm okay." I hated that Monique was so concerned for me. "Jorge would never let me get hurt. If something happens to me he loses half the stories that he tells Linda."

Jorge's wife, Linda, was a US Marine who was deployed overseas. I had been made aware that Jorge kept her entertained with stories of my antics. I was pretty confident that having a front row seat to those stories was the main reason he was so willing to work with me.

"Be careful, ma petite."

"I always try to be," I said quietly.

"I know," she sighed.

After hanging up I turned and found Griffin watching me with a concerned look on his face.

"Problems?" he asked.

I put a smile on my face. "Nothing I can't handle."

"You sure?"

"Of course I'm sure." I could tell he was worried so I tried changing the subject. "How's Ramos?"

Griffin looked pained. "She doesn't sound like she's doing so great."

He looked lost as if he didn't know how to fix this for her. The fact he cared so much reminded me why I loved him.

"Do you want to go see how she's doing?" I asked.

"I can stay here with you if you have a problem."

I shook my head. "I don't have a problem. Monique's having a little bit of fun with staffing at the moment but she'll work it out. She always does."

"If you're sure."

I nodded. "At this moment Ramos needs you far more than I do. I know she's hurting."

Griffin pulled me into his arms and kissed me on the top of the head. "You're amazing, you know that? Fletchall's a jerk but he was right about that."

I looked up and kissed him softly. "I'll see you when you get back."

He nodded and reluctantly let me go. "Shouldn't be too late."

Chapter Eleven

The apartment was quiet without Griffin in it. I was becoming used to having his presence dominating the small space. A knock on the door interrupted my silence. Opening it, I found Crystal and Edwin with pizza boxes.

"We were wondering whether you would like dinner with us."

I eyed off the pizza. "I can see you put effort into it."

"Are you going to criticize or do you want food?" Crystal queried. "At least we're trying. We could have just turned up and expected you to feed us."

That was true, it had happened often enough in the past.

Once settled at the table I turned to Crystal. "How was your day with your mom?"

Crystal surprised me by smiling. "It went really well. I met John."

"What's he like?" I asked.

"Picture the man that you would have expected my mom to pick based on the last thirty years of her life," Crystal said.

"Okay."

"Now imagine somebody who is the complete opposite of that image. That is John."

"Really?"

"Yes, really. Wait here a minute."

I watched as Crystal raced out of my apartment.

I looked over at Edwin who was devouring far more pizza than you would expect for a man who prided himself on his toned physique.

"She seems excited."

Edwin nodded, looking slightly worried. "She is. I'm kind of a little surprised. Considering what she'd told me about her mother, I figured she had given up on a normal mother-daughter relationship. It looks like it was something that she really wanted. I'm trying to keep an eye on things. I'm just worried that there is something else behind this. Considering the stories that Crystal has told me, I'm having a little trouble believing that the woman has made that much of a change in her life. Crystal's dad is a bit concerned as well."

"How's he coping with the whole thing?"

"You know George. Whatever makes his little girl happy is fine with him. I can tell he's a little worried though." Edwin looked around surreptitiously. "He's having Roxy and John investigated. So far they haven't found anything but George doesn't want to be taken by surprise. Crystal doesn't know."

That was not good. "Crystal is going to lose it if she finds out that her father is going behind her back."

"That is why no one is going to tell her about it."

"Why did you tell me then? I don't want to be keeping anything from her."

"Because he told me and I'm feeling guilty that I haven't told her so I need someone else to share in that guilt." Edwin did look torn.

"Well, thanks for that," I grumbled.

Crystal walked back into the apartment with her phone.

"I got some photos today of John and his family. Seems I'm going to be getting a stepbrother and two stepsisters."

She passed the phone to me and I started scrolling through the photos. John and his family looked surprisingly normal.

"So, John lives in LA?" I asked.

Crystal nodded as she dug into a slice of pizza. "He met Roxy on a holiday in Vegas a few months ago. Seems they've been pretty inseparable since then. Love at first sight from what they've been telling me."

"Is your mom going to be moving here or will John

move to Vegas?"

"Roxy is going to be moving here. She said that her husband and daughter live here so it is obviously the place that she should be."

I glanced at Edwin and I could see that my concern was reflected in his eyes as well. Crystal seemed to be embracing the change in her mother a lot more eagerly than either of us was expecting.

"You're taking things slowly, aren't you?" I asked, hoping I wasn't going to upset her.

Crystal stopped eating and stared at me. "Of course I'm taking it slowly." Her gaze softened as she looked between Edwin and me, taking in our concerned expressions. "I'm not an idiot," she said softly. "I know the kind of woman Roxy is, I'm not going into this blindly. I'll be careful but it's kind of nice to have a bit of a normal family for a change."

"Okay," I said. "I'm just worried about you. You know me. I'm not fully comfortable with life unless I'm worrying about somebody."

Crystal chuckled. "That reminds me. My mom wants you and Griffin at the wedding."

I stopped the pizza heading for my mouth. "Why? I don't know the woman. Why on Earth would she want me at her wedding?"

"I think she felt bad for the way she spoke to you today at the dress shop."

I raised an eyebrow. "Did you not explain to her the industry I work in? I have had far worse things said to me in my lifetime. Come to think of it, some of those worse things came from you," I said, gesturing to Crystal.

"Ha ha. Very funny. I think she knows how good a friend of mine that you are and she is trying to get on my good side."

"Oh, so not a real invitation. It's one of those second thought invitations where there is some convoluted reasoning for inviting someone to the wedding, usually when someone else has declined their invite."

Crystal looked at me sourly. "Stop over thinking it. You and Griffin are invited. It will be a nice night out for you where you are not working for a change."

Crystal was right. Most of my social outings were to do with work. This meant they involved trying to prevent celebrities from doing something extraordinarily stupid that could end up in the media within minutes. Not always a fun job. In fact, not ever a fun job.

I shrugged. "Sure. I'll need to check with Griffin but I don't think he'll be back at work by then, so we should both be free."

"Is Griffin taking a holiday?" Edwin asked curiously.

I shook my head. "He's been kind of suspended."

Crystal stopped eating. "How do you get 'kind of' suspended?"

"Seems Griffin and his lieutenant aren't seeing eye to eye on the investigation into Ramos's girlfriend's death. Griffin dealt with it in his usual subtle way so he's been forced to take some overdue leave.

"He really doesn't have people skills, does he?" said Edwin.

I shook my head. "Not even close. I'd hate to see him in a job where he actually has to think of the most diplomatic way to phrase something before he starts speaking."

"How long is this forced holiday going to be for?" asked Edwin.

I shrugged. "I don't know. Hopefully not too long. I don't think that Griffin would be very good with too much time on his hands. I hate to think what kind of trouble he could get himself into."

Chapter Twelve

Walking into the mansion the next day, I was not surprised to find that things were exactly the same as they had been before the discovery of Jolena's body. For some reason I always had the feeling that the world should stop when someone dies, but it never does. As usual, the guys in the band were still in bed. First thing in the morning it was always the staff who were around, ensuring everything was going to run smoothly during the day. I had received a phone call the night before letting me know that there was going to be a meeting first thing in the morning. It looked like management wanted to make sure that everyone was on the same page. I went looking for Jorge. No matter how early I arrived at work, he was always there earlier. When I found Jorge in the living room I was surprised to find him talking to Griffin. I hadn't heard from Griffin since receiving a text the night before, letting me know that he wasn't going to be able to come over to my place and he would be crashing at his home for a change.

"Detective Griffin, I wasn't expecting to see you back at work so soon."

Griffin grinned nervously. Jorge looked pained. That combination of expressions did not bode well.

"What's going on?" I asked cautiously.

"I'm not here for work," said Griffin, "at least not police work."

Jorge cleared his throat. "Detective Griffin has been hired by Monique to act as security for the band."

"Really?"

Griffin smiled widely. "It'll be great. You and I can work together. I've got to check in with management to go through my duties but I'll see you after."

He gave me a quick kiss and left me standing in the middle of the living room, struggling to deal with what had just happened.

"You need to breathe," Jorge said, waving a hand in front of my face. "Seriously, Trudie. Just take one breath."

I dropped down on the couch and put my head between my knees, trying to reestablish control over my lungs. I turned my head and looked at Jorge who had squatted down next to me.

"This is not good, this is so not good."

Jorge awkwardly patted me on the knee. "It isn't that bad. Monique would never have put him into this job if she didn't think he could cope with it."

"It isn't that," I moaned. "I can't work with Griffin, we can't work together. We have very defined boundaries in our relationship. I bought one of those flat pack desks for my apartment one weekend and we tried to put it together. Seven hours it took us and in the end we were only able to do it when he went out for a walk before we killed each other. In the twenty minutes he was gone I managed to assemble it. We can't even cook a meal together. He cooks it or I cook it. We don't do it together."

Jorge looked stunned. "Why can't you cook a meal together?"

"Because he cuts the vegetables the wrong shape and I refuse to follow a recipe," I said, glaring at him. I knew full well how I sounded.

Jorge sat back on his heels. "I think I'm seeing a bit of your crazy side," he said.

"Yes you are and it is a side of myself that I usually keep hidden from the people I work with. Griffin is the only one who gets to see my crazy side. If he's here then that brings my crazy side into the workplace. I can't have that happening. What on Earth was Monique thinking?"

Jorge shrugged, trying to look understanding. Of course that was ruined by the fact that I could see he wanted to burst out laughing at my predicament. "Maybe she was desperate. She couldn't find anyone else."

"But she should know not to do something like this to me. If she didn't think it was going to be a problem she would have called me. She knew how bad an idea this was. That's why she didn't say anything." I could feel myself getting angry.

"You know, we've all been thinking that you're the saint for putting up with Griffin. I'm kind of reevaluating my opinion of him," Jorge said, smiling widely.

"That's just great," I grumbled.

"Maybe you should speak to Monique directly," Jorge said quietly, obviously trying desperately to remove himself from the equation.

I pulled my phone out of my bag while wondering how I was going to tell the woman I admired most in the world that she had just made the worst decision ever.

I didn't have to wait long for her to answer.

"Trudie, ma petite, what can I do for you this beautiful morning?"

Oh, she knew I was not going to be happy with this. That was just too cheery a greeting to be genuine.

"Did you want to explain to me why Griffin now has a job working security with Jorge?" I asked, deciding that small talk was beyond what I was capable of today.

"I was having some trouble filling the second security spot and I became aware that Detective Griffin was available for a short-term security position."

I wasn't even going to bother asking how Monique had learned that Griffin had been suspended. She seemed to know what was happening in this town before the rest of the world did.

"How were you even able to get him permission to work here? His lieutenant would have a fit if he knew he was here."

"Oh, that wasn't a problem. Lieutenant Ellis was surprisingly accommodating and gave permission immediately," Monique said airily.

I hung my head. Of course he did. Silly me, I should have known that hoping for a man with the ability to say no to Monique was more than the universe was willing to give me.

"And management here, how did they react to the news that their new security guy was a cop?"

"A lot of security people these days are serving police officers. It is common for them to take second jobs. Policing is not exactly a highly paid profession."

I waited, wondering what else she had to say.

"I did tell you that I was having trouble filling the position. When Detective Griffin contacted me and suggested that he work as a secondary security person, it just seemed to be the perfect answer to our little dilemma."

It was far from perfect but I had a feeling that I had been played.

"I have impressed on Griffin that both he and Jorge are answerable to you. If you are really unhappy with the situation I will fire him for you if you want."

I could hear the query in Monique's voice as if she was curious how I was going to react to that offer. I will admit that there was a small part of me that was tempted to remove this situation before it became a major problem. But that wasn't the kind of person that I was.

I sighed heavily. "No, I'll deal with it."

"Of course you will, ma petite. I have complete confidence in you."

I wish I did because I had a feeling this was not a situation that was going to end well.

I turned off my phone and glared at Jorge for no reason other than that he was there.

"So, we're a happy threesome, are we?" he said.

"Yes we are," I replied through gritted teeth, "and could you please not refer to us as a threesome. This situation is difficult enough without you throwing that word into the mix."

Jorge grimaced. "I see your point."

I was still wondering how the best way to deal with the situation was when Griffin walked confidently back into the room.

Jorge muttered out an excuse and beat a hasty retreat.

"So," Griffin drawled, "have you spoken to Monique yet to find out whether this is all some horrible mistake?"

"Yes, I have and I don't know why you're doing this but for some reason she is supporting you."

"I'm not trying to make your life difficult," Griffin said softly.

"And yet you're doing a great job of it," I said. I took in a deep breath. "No, wait. I shouldn't have said that. I've just been blindsided and I'm not dealing with it well."

"I know, probably the reason I was too chicken to tell you last night. I heard you on the phone to Monique and knew she was having trouble getting security for this job. I called her and offered to take the position."

"How did you convince Monique to give you this job?" I asked suspiciously.

Griffin gave me a boyish grin. "I charmed her," he said confidently.

"Oh, honey," I said. "I know you remember. Charm is not one of your strengths."

Griffin's face fell at my frank assessment of his personality. I wasn't worried. I was being honest and it only took Griffin a second's contemplation before he realized it.

"Why else would she have given me the job?" he asked.

I wasn't sure but I had my suspicions. Monique wasn't overly fond of Griffin and had made her quiet opposition to our relationship quite obvious. I wouldn't put it past her to be putting a little pressure on the relationship, just to see how it reacted. I could see I needed to have a word with my boss regarding boundaries at some point.

"Are you here to investigate Jolena's death?" I asked.

Griffin shook his head. "No, I am under strict orders not to do any investigating. Fletchall and Pickett are doing that and there is no way I want to interfere. It's more important to me that the case be handled strictly according to the law. When they find whoever did this I do not want anything getting in the way of a clean conviction."

And that was what made Griffin a good cop.

"Then why are you here?" I asked.

"Monique really wanted backup for Jorge. She's worried about you. Jorge's worried about you. Everyone's worried about you. Most of the time I can't protect you because we are living such separate lives. For this one moment I can make sure that you are safe. That means more to me than my career, more than finding Jolena's killer, more than anything."

The cold lump of nerves in my stomach melted at his words.

"Okay." I took in a deep breath. "We can do this. We just need to respect each other. You need to remember that this is my career and that we work as a team, but I get final say."

Griffin nodded, not what I would call enthusiastically but I was willing to take what I could get.

"Do you want a coffee?" I asked.

Griffin nodded again, obviously unwilling to say anything else while I was in my current mood. I led him to the kitchen and wanted to cry when I found Buddy chewing on a wooden bar stool with great relish.

Griffin peered over my shoulder at the scene in front of us.

"Trudie, why is there a goat in the kitchen?" Griffin asked.

"I really don't think you want to know," I said.

"Is there something happening here that I need to report to someone?"

I snorted. "Believe me, that goat is treated better than I am."

Griffin fixed me with that stare of his. "Honey, I know how some of your clients treat you. That statement does not fill me with confidence."

Buddy chose that moment to look up and bleat at me balefully.

"He doesn't seem to like you," Griffin contributed unhelpfully.

"I already worked that out," I grumbled as I dropped my purse on the bench. "I'm going to need some help with this."

Griffin looked at me doubtfully. "I'm not sure this comes under security."

"You know, I never get this sort of lip from Jorge." Luckily for me, Jorge wasn't around to point out the obvious inaccuracy of that statement. "He knows not to question me when I tell him that wrestling a goat into a pen comes under our list of duties," I said sourly.

Griffin raised an eyebrow. "Whatever you say, boss."

Chapter Thirteen

Once we had managed to convince a reluctant Buddy that there were far better eating options in his pen than the wooden legs of a kitchen bar stool, Griffin and I found our way to the morning meeting. The staff for the band was relatively small considering how many people most celebrities had to cater to their every whim. We wandered over and sat next to Jorge who eyed us suspiciously.

"Have a few problems with Buddy, did we?"

"How did you know?" I asked.

"Goat hair," Jorge said as he picked something off my pants.

I looked down at myself and, sure enough, I did seem to be sporting a growth of goat hair.

"Wonderful," I muttered as I started wiping as much of the hair off myself as I could.

I looked over at Griffin. Somehow he had managed to remain goat hair free. I wouldn't put it past Buddy to have found a way to make his hair stick to me on purpose.

I was so busy trying to clean myself up that I didn't notice when the meeting started. The manager introduced Harold O'Brien, the lawyer who had rescued me from the best interrogation I had ever had.

I looked up with a smile on my face, only to have it freeze when I saw that Harold was not alone.

"As you are all aware, Jolena Aaron died two days ago and her body was found on this property. The police are currently investigating the unfortunate death of this young lady. After spending yesterday in discussions with the band and management, it has been decided that extra staff are required." He indicated the new arrival beside him. "Mr Travis Cooper will be evaluating security on the property and for the band. I hope that you will all provide him with your complete cooperation."

Travis's gaze swept the small group. He smiled at me and when he spotted Griffin sitting next to me, a mischievous glint entered his eyes.

"I need you to keep an eye out and if anything looks out of place I need you to speak to Mr Cooper immediately."

The murmur of assent from the staff seemed to satisfy the lawyer. I sneaked a glance over to Griffin and wasn't surprised to find he had put on his blank cop face. Griffin and Travis had a complicated relationship which had only just started to thaw, kind of. The fact that Travis was going to be evaluating Griffin in his new, hopefully very temporary, job did not look like it was going to help their fractured relationship.

Harold looked over in our direction, disapproval in his expression when his gaze landed on Griffin.

"Mr Griffin, may I have a word?"

Griffin nodded sharply and followed the lawyer out of the room.

I watched him leave with a worried expression on my face. Now that I had accepted that Griffin was going to be working with me, I was a bit concerned that the lawyer was going to put an end to our little experiment. Sighing, I looked around and caught Travis's eyes as he was talking to a staff member who had cornered him. Travis winked at me over his head.

"Miss Eyre," he called out. "I think I'll be seeing you first. Could you please meet me in the front study in five minutes?"

I nodded my assent and turned towards Jorge.

"I cut a nun off in traffic on my way to work, didn't I?"

"Why do you say that?" asked Jorge.

"Because nothing else could explain why I'm being punished this way," I said morosely.

"Really not dealing with today well, are you, cupcake?"

"I had just got my head around the fact that I was going to be working with Griffin. I was handling it, maybe not particularly well, but I was handling it. Now I have got to deal with Travis and that is generally not what I would consider the best part of my day."

"You just need to be positive," Jorge smiled encouragingly.

"You know, you sound like you're giving me good advice. The words are there. But I'm seeing an evil grin on your face as if you are trying to make sure you remember everything so you won't miss anything when you recount this story to Linda."

Jorge nodded enthusiastically. "I may need a pen and some paper so I can take notes though. I have a feeling that this is going to be a bumper day."

That was just great.

I knocked on the door of the study. When I heard Travis calling out for me to enter, I walked in.

Travis looked up from the desk he had obviously claimed as his own and smiled when he saw me. "Griffin is working here?"

Of course that was how we were going to start. "Don't say a word."

"You and Griffin are working together?"

"Please, just stop talking."

"Oh, this is going to be priceless. I may just tell them I'm working for free, just to get the chance to watch you two together."

"Are you quite finished?" I asked.

Travis nodded. "Sure. Would it be tasteless of me to tape the exact moment when your relationship implodes?"

"I thought you and Griffin had talked and sorted out all your problems," I said.

"We grabbed a beer and watched a game. He may have also given me a free shot at punching him. That was pretty much it."

"So now that you've made up in a quintessentially guy

fashion, why are you still giving me grief?" I asked.

"Even when I was partnered with him we weren't really what you would call best buds. He's a little uptight, follows the rules a little too strictly. I had days when I just wanted to kill the man. At least I got to go home at the end of the day where I could calm down from the joy of dealing with him. You don't even have that, do you?"

Travis looked smug as if he was reading a playbook of the future of my relationship.

"We'll be fine," I said, even though I didn't for one second believe that.

Travis laughed with a disbelieving look on his face. "Sure you'll be fine. Grab a seat, will you. I have to say I was quite surprised when I found out that you and I would be working together again."

"We are not working together. I am doing my job over here and you are doing your job way over there. There may be times when we need to speak to each other but that is the extent of our working together." There was no way that I was going to get caught between Travis and Griffin again. "So are you going to tell me why you are here? I'm having a little trouble believing that you have been hired for an evaluation of security. And since fidelity isn't exactly a highly prized commodity around here, I don't really think that you have been hired on a cheating case."

A ghost of a smile flitted across Travis's lips. "The management company has some concerns that a crime like this occurred so close to the band. Naturally, one of those concerns is that it may be a member of the band who is responsible."

"Isn't that a job for the police?"

Travis nodded. "I'm not here to build a case for or against anyone. I am here to see what I can find out and provide management with a heads up in case this isn't a random murder that can be laid at someone else's feet. They want to have time to prepare for any contingency."

"So to clarify, they want you to find out who was most

likely to have killed Jolena so they can put in place a course of action which will cause the least amount of damage to the brand."

Travis nodded.

As usual when faced with the machinations of the Hollywood system, I felt the very real need to have a shower.

"No one really cares about Jolena anymore, do they?"

Travis shook his head. "You know how it works, Trudie."

"What will you do with the information if you find it before the cops?"

Travis stiffened. "I won't let them cover it up. If one of the band did this, I'll be reporting it to Fletchall and Pickett. They won't get away with it."

I should have known. Despite my initial suspicions, I knew that Travis was a cop at heart.

I clasped my hands primly in my lap. "So, Mr Cooper, how may I help you today?"

Travis smiled slowly. "Just wanting to get my head around the situation. I've got the band's version of events and the manager has spoken to me, but I've got a bit of a feeling that I may not be getting the whole story. What do you think about the guys in the band?"

"I like them for the most part. They're fun to be around and they're pretty nice guys."

"Really?" Travis asked. "You're trying to tell me that five men who are in a rock band and have some of the worst reputations on the planet for the way they break women's hearts are really misunderstood nice guys. Even with your ability to ignore reality and see the best in people, I would think that is stretching the truth a bit far."

"I will admit that the first week with them was a little rough," I conceded. "They treated me the same way that they have a tendency to treat everyone, not just women. I think the guys have bought into the whole rock and roll lifestyle and they think that behaving badly is a part of that.

After they met Griffin and they understood that I was in a committed relationship things changed and they started treating me with a measure of respect."

Travis eyed me doubtfully.

"What?"

"You are expecting me to believe that all it took was Griffin walking in and they started respecting your relationship boundaries."

I nodded.

"Having a little trouble with that one, sweetheart."

I shrugged. "What do you want me to say? That's the way it happened. Griffin picked me up and then the guys just wanted to talk and be friends. Frankly, I think they are so used to women throwing themselves at them and expecting things from them that they are grateful to have someone that they can just talk to. Someone with no expectations of them living up to the rock and roll lifestyle."

Travis still looked doubtful. There wasn't much I could say to that. Even if the guys had never met Griffin I would most likely have ended up in this position. In most circumstances I invariably ended up as one of the guys. I'd had that effect on males all my life. It was a gift.

"Tell me a bit about each of the band members."

"What do you want to know?"

"Just your impressions."

"Okay," I said slowly. "Vale is the drummer and seems to be the nicest of the guys. From what I understand he grew up in a small town and met the others when he came to LA. I haven't really seen Vale party to the same extent as the others. I know he has a bit of a reputation when he is on tour but I haven't really seen evidence of it. Dion is the lead guitarist and he and Sewell, the bass player, are pretty tight. If one of them is involved in something, the other one is right behind him. They are both a bit wild with the parties and they do have a tendency to wind up the rest of the band. Tim is on keyboard and he is the smart one of the group. Financially, he is an absolute genius. I can see the rest of the band losing everything within five years of Crispy Spider breaking up but Tim will be rich for the rest of his life. While the others are buying lots of cars and spending money on women and whatever else they spend the money on, Tim invests his and he is by far in a much better place than the rest of the guys." I paused as I tried to work out what to say next.

"What about Ash?" Travis asked when I'd let the silence go on too long.

"Ash is a bit different to the others. He's the lead singer so that puts him at center stage for everything. He is the one that gets the most attention and he is also the one that cops the most blame when the band does something wild or stupid. Usually stupid. He doesn't really care what people say about him and he definitely goes his own way."

"There's something else, isn't there?"

I should have known that Travis would pick up on my hesitation when discussing Ash.

"Ever heard of the 27 Club?"

Travis nodded. "Isn't that what they call the curse that seems to hit musicians that die at the age of twenty-seven? There seems to have been a few of them."

"Well, Ash has got it into his head that he is going to become a member of the 27 Club."

"He thinks he's going to die?"

I nodded. "I don't know whether he thinks he is going to die. It could be more that he believes he is destined to be a legend."

I could see Travis rolling his eyes. I would have thought that a private investigator would be better at hiding his feelings about his client's little quirks.

"He is twenty-six now and he lives his life like the clock is running down at a breakneck speed. Ash will try anything once. A lot of the trouble that the band seems to get into can be directly related back to Ash's belief that his time is running out."

"Would that be why he had a threesome with Jolena?"

I shook my head. "No, that was a normal part of life for these guys. They're young men in their twenties and very few people are willing to say no to them. Women throwing themselves at them constantly is just another part of their normal day."

"You've never been tempted?" queried Travis.

I looked at him sourly. "Of course I haven't. I'm with Griffin. I'm not going to throw that away on some meaningless encounter."

"Aah, loyalty. I know it exists, I just never get to see it in action," Travis grinned.

"That is the saddest thing that you have ever said to me. How can you live your life with that level of cynicism?"

Travis shrugged. "I'm not exactly in an industry that sees the finest in human nature. I find it amazing that you work in a similar environment but you are not just as cynical as I am."

I smiled. "I may not have the best examples of humanity in my work life but I have the best this world has to offer in my personal life. Maybe you should look at that."

Travis looked uncomfortable. "Back to the subject at hand, do you think that Ash might have gone too far with an experience with Jolena?"

I shook my head. "Ash is pretty controlled about what he does. I don't see him accidentally killing Jolena."

"What if it wasn't an accident? Maybe it could have been one of those things that Ash wanted to experience before he meets his legendary end."

"You mean a thrill killing?"

I wasn't overly fond of Ash but I couldn't really see him doing that.

"It happens," Travis said. "This guy has got pretty much everything that money could buy and a perceived time limit. This usually turns people from buying things to having experiences. Murder for some people is just another experience."

"Did you know that Jolena was Ramos's girlfriend?" I asked.

That pulled Travis up short. "No, I hadn't been told that."

"You need to remember that. Whatever you find out is going to have a direct impact on her. You might want to be sensitive when it comes to your theories."

Travis nodded. "Thanks, Trudie. I'll keep that in mind."

"I hope you do. Ramos is in a lot of pain at the moment. First, Jolena dies. Then she finds out that she was cheating on her. No matter how strong a person is, that is going to have an effect."

"I understand. Anything else you have that might help me with looking into this."

I shook my head. "The whole thing seemed so random. There was no indication that something like this was going to happen. As far as assignments go, this one has been relatively easy. Because the band is in lockdown there hasn't been many of the usual chances for things to go as badly as they usually do when dealing with celebrities. At least we haven't had problems with paparazzi for a change."

"Any tried to get on the property?"

I shook my head. "In the beginning we had a few camped out the front, waiting for the band to hit the town or to see whether any famous women turned up for the parties. But the guys have been smart. Generally, the women who get invited aren't well known. It keeps everything a lot more low key than it usually would."

"Sounds very well thought out and cozy," Travis said.

"Crispy Spider's last album didn't do as well as was expected. Their antics on their latest tour kind of took away from the music. The sales were good but they weren't great. The management company stepped in and laid down the law. This business is ruthless. You don't produce amazing sales, there is always someone else nipping at your heels. Luckily, the guys heard what was being said and that's why this little retreat was organized. We keep them as cloistered as possible and give them the chance to create with as few distractions as we possibly can."

Travis looked skeptical. "Parties with hot women every night does not exactly sound very cloistered to me."

I recognized the truth in that statement. "For these guys it was the best compromise we could come up with. The idea is that if it is kept in-house then security can deal with any issues that may eventuate. It keeps the situation from getting messy."

"Didn't exactly go to plan, did it?"

"No," I said, "it didn't."

"I'm going to need you to take me through everything that happened that morning," Travis said as he stood up. "If I can walk through what you did and what you saw, I may get a better handle on it."

I stood up and absentmindedly brush at some more of the goat hair that was stubbornly refusing to leave me. "Not a problem. Just do me a favor and try not to antagonize Griffin."

Travis gave me his trademark grin. "Of course, Trudie. I'll be on my best behavior."

That just filled me with confidence.

Chapter Fourteen

I followed Travis through the door. I wasn't surprised to find Griffin waiting for us.

"Griffin," Travis nodded.

"Cooper," Griffin replied.

I waited a second as both of them eyed each other.

"Seriously, guys. We're doing this now?"

Griffin broke eye contact first.

"No, you're right. We need to act professional. Cooper and I have worked together before…"

"And wasn't that just a special experience?" Travis interrupted.

I rolled my eyes. I seriously could not believe that I had to put up with this. It was like two irritating puppies fighting for dominance.

"We have a job to do and we all need to work together, nicely," I said through gritted teeth. I was very much looking forward to the end of this day.

Griffin at least had the ability to look a little shamefaced. "Sorry, instinctive reaction."

"You need to work on those," I muttered.

"Still can't believe you got a job here," pointed out Travis.

"You're not the only one," Griffin said tightly.

I shot a worried look in his direction. "Is everything okay?"

Griffin nodded. "The lawyer is not happy that I'm here but he was overruled by management. Seems Monique has a lot of say when she wants it."

I nodded. We were all just lucky that Monique used her powers for good rather than evil. If she ever went to the dark side, the world could be in real trouble.

"So, what are you two doing now?" asked Griffin suspiciously.

"I'm walking Travis through what I did the other morning when I found Jolena's body."

"Do you mind if I tag along?"

"Sure," I said.

"Don't you have work you're supposed to be doing?" queried Travis.

Griffin shrugged. "Nobody seems to have any idea what to do with me. I have been given strict instructions to stay away from the band. Seems the lawyer doesn't trust me not to bust them on a drugs charge or something."

To be perfectly honest, neither did I.

"Monique wanted me to stay close to you and be there if Jorge needs help, so that is what I'm going to do," Griffin said with a smile on his face.

I couldn't really say that I found that smile to be comforting at all.

"Is Trudie in danger?" interrupted Travis.

I was touched by the concern in his voice. Griffin obviously heard it as well because he frowned at his former partner.

"Some of us are just a little worried about Trudie."

"That would be a full-time job," muttered Travis.

"Hey," I said. "I'm fine if you insist on taking pot shots at Griffin here but could we please keep me out of the line of fire."

Travis grinned widely.

"Don't try looking innocent with me. I know you too well for that to work," I warned.

Travis shrugged. "So, what were you doing when you first got to work that morning?"

"Well, when I got to the mansion I went to check on Buddy because he's been causing problems for us lately. I just wanted to make sure he was contained."

Travis looked startled as he followed me through the house with Griffin trailing behind.

"Who is Buddy and why exactly does he need to be contained?"

"Hasn't anyone told you about Buddy yet?" I asked.

Travis shook his head.

"Oh, Travis, you are in for a treat."

"I really don't think you mean that in the way I'm hoping you mean that," Travis said wryly.

I laughed as I led the two men to Buddy's pen, grateful that, for once, the goat was exactly where he was supposed to be.

"This is Buddy," I said with a flourish.

Buddy glared at me. I wish I knew what I had done to make this goat hate me so much. It might have to do with the fact that my job description seemed to be to thwart him at every turn.

"It's a goat," Travis said.

"Yes, it's a goat. He's Vale's pet. Unfortunately he is a bit of an escape artist and on the day Jolena died he had managed to get out of his pen. That's the reason I was down near the lake. I had looked through the house and the grounds and I found him there."

Travis and Griffin followed me as I headed to the lake. I was surprised to see Vale there and indicated to the others to stay back.

"Are you okay, Vale?" I asked tentatively as I stood next to him.

Vale looked startled. "Trudie, I didn't know whether you'd be back here. I thought everything that happened might have scared you away."

I shook my head. "It generally takes a lot more than that to chase me away from a job. I survived the first week with you guys so I figure that I can pretty much get through anything."

Vale gave me a tight smile. "I'm sorry we were so painful. I should have realized from the start that you didn't deserve to be treated like that. I think we were just so annoyed that we were being locked down like we were that you were the easiest target."

"Not the first time it's happened," I said. "Although I have to say it was close. I think I still have the resignation letter on file that I started. It wasn't very complimentary to you guys."

Vale gave me a half smile. "I'm sure it wasn't. I'm also sure that we deserved everything that you said. I'm glad you decided to stay."

'Thanks," I said. "I'm glad I stayed as well. What are you doing out here?"

Vale looked sadly across the lake. "Just seems to be a huge waste. Sometimes I wonder what I'm even doing here. I always thought that I was going to change the world and leave it a better place. I don't quite think that I'm accomplishing that goal."

"You're definitely making an impact on it," I said gently. "Have you thought about using the influence that you now have for a cause you are interested in? You have the opportunity to really make a difference if that is what you want to do."

Vale nodded. "I think you might be right. We got so caught up in making it as a band that I think we may have lost part of ourselves."

"It doesn't have to be that way."

I wondered where this sudden introspection was coming from. It looked like the events of the last few days were starting to take a toll on Vale. There was nothing like a murder to start you questioning your place in the world.

"I think you're right." Vale paused as if gathering his thoughts. "You know that you are very easy to talk to?"

"I've been told that often," I said wryly.

"I don't think you realize what a gift that is," he said reflectively. He looked out across the lake again. "What are you doing down here anyway, Trudie?"

I motioned towards Travis and Griffin who were standing a relatively respectful distance behind us. "We have new security people and we were just going over the issues from the last couple of days."

Vale frowned. "Isn't that your boyfriend?" he asked, with a slightly accusing tone.

"Yes, he is. He was available for security work and my boss thought he would be helpful."

Vale looked skeptical. I wasn't going to argue with him. I still had my doubts about this arrangement. Now that I'd had Travis thrown into the mix, I was just going to keep my head down until this entire job was finished.

Vale grabbed my elbow and pulled me aside to where he thought that the two men wouldn't be able to hear us. I didn't have the heart to tell him I knew for a fact that Griffin had the hearing of a bat.

"I don't think that is entirely appropriate," Vale said quietly.

I looked down pointedly at the way Vale was still gripping my elbow.

"Sorry," he muttered as he let go.

"It's all been approved by management." I was a little confused by the annoyance I could see on Vale's face.

"I think I need to have a little talk to them about that."

I stayed silent. I didn't really see Vale's reasoned argument beating Monique's powers of persuasion but I wasn't going to try to stop him.

Vale smiled at me as if trying to hide his annoyance. "I'm really glad you came back," he said, before turning and walking away.

I watched him worriedly as he walked towards the mansion. I kept watching him as I heard Griffin and Travis step up behind me.

"He likes you," Griffin said accusingly.

I tried to control my impatience before turning to face the two of them.

"Of course he likes me. Unlike you, I'm a very likable person."

"You know what I mean."

I took a deep breath. "I know that you have this belief

that just because you find me irresistible that every other man in the world must feel the same way. Here's a newsflash for you. They don't. Vale is just being nice to me. New concept amongst my clients but the law of averages said I had to hit one sooner or later."

"Griffin's right," Travis decided to interfere. "I think he does like you."

I turned around to face the newest attack. "You might want to think on what you just said. I never thought that I would hear you say the words 'Griffin is right' without you choking on it or at least a threat of imminent death."

Travis grimaced. "I know. Believe me they were just as unpleasant for me to say as they were for you to hear. Doesn't stop them from being the truth."

I shrugged, giving up. One thing I had learned very quickly about the people I seemed to attract into my life, they were not easily swayed when they had an opinion.

"This was where I found Buddy. I was talking to Crystal on the phone when I spotted him."

"Why were you talking to Crystal?" Travis asked curiously.

"We were discussing how ridiculous my life had become when I was required to spend my working hours hunting down a goat who, as we've already seen, does not like me."

"Okay." Travis drawled, attempting to be understanding.

"I got off the phone with Crystal and I was trying to reason with Buddy."

"We're still talking about the goat?" Travis queried.

"Yes, we are still talking about the goat. I was not going to be able to drag him all the way back to his pen on my own so I was trying to discuss the matter calmly with him. He wasn't exactly responding to my reasoned arguments and I looked out over the lake because I was feeling a little frustrated with the situation." I paused for a moment as I remembered that morning. "I saw some fabric in the lake, a lot of fabric. I ditched my phone and went in to see what it was."

"Why?" asked Travis.

"Why, what?" I replied.

"You see fabric in a lake. Why did you decide to jump fully clothed in a lake when all you'd seen was fabric?"

I shrugged. "I don't know. I just got a bad feeling. I guess I reacted without thinking. I swam out to it and grabbed hold. It was only then that I knew that it was a person. I dragged her to the shore and tried doing CPR. I started screaming for someone to come and help me. Jorge heard me and came running. When he got there he realized that there was nothing that we could do to help her so he stopped me. I was a bit of a mess so Jorge took over from there. He organized everyone and called 911."

"Why were you so upset?" Travis asked curiously.

"I'd just pulled a dead body out of the water," I replied, wondering why I had thought that for once Travis would show some sensitivity.

"I understand that but it wasn't exactly your first time finding a dead body. You're usually pretty good with dealing with it. What made this one different?"

"I'd met Jolena the day before at a barbecue for some of the cops from the station. When I pulled her out of the lake I knew who she was. I knew what this was going to do to Ramos."

"So why was Jolena here?" asked Travis.

"She was here a few nights earlier," I offered.

"Yes, I heard about the incident. I've already spoken to Ash. He claims that she was nothing more than some random fan that he didn't even know or care about."

That was Ash. Classy to the end.

"How much did Ramos know about Jolena and her extracurricular activities?" Travis asked.

I looked at Griffin who cleared his throat.

"Trudie told me about Jolena when we got home after the barbecue. I was planning on telling Ramos."

"Brave man," Travis commented.

Griffin raised an eyebrow.

Travis grimaced. "As the man who regularly gets to tell people that their significant other is cheating on them, believe me when I say that it is not a job for the faint of heart. People have a tendency to react badly and as the messenger you are the first in the line of fire."

"Probably true," Griffin conceded. "I'll admit that I wasn't looking forward to the discussion. I was still trying to work out a way to approach her about it when we got the call that a woman's body had been found here. I was concerned as I knew Trudie was the only woman working here so I didn't get a chance to tell her. It was only after things calmed down that I filled her in on what Trudie told me."

"Why?" asked Travis.

"There was no way that I was going to let Marty Fletchall give her that piece of information during the course of his investigation."

Travis frowned. "They still don't get along?"

Griffin shook his head. "The two of them just don't have anything to do with each other but I wouldn't put it past him to give her that news in the worst way possible. I didn't want her to have to deal with that on top of everything else."

"She didn't know beforehand, had no indication?"

Griffin shrugged. "She may have had some suspicions, but she didn't know. She did say that Jolena had been planning on catching up with an old friend but hadn't given Ramos any indication as to who it was."

Travis turned back to me. "Was there anyone else up at that time, someone hanging around that you didn't expect to see?"

"Ash was up when I got here," I remembered. "He was smoking near Buddy's pen. It was strange because the one thing that is consistent with these guys is that they are night owls. They party all night and usually they don't get out of bed until mid-morning at the very earliest. Being awake when I got here would be counted as a very early morning for Ash. I don't think it had happened once while I've been here."

"Interesting," said Travis.

"Interesting? That's all you've got to say about it. He could have killed Jolena."

Travis looked surprised. "This is new. I thought you were always convinced your client couldn't have possibly killed the victim. I would usually expect you to go into some kind of impassioned defense of Ash."

"Not today," I said. "I've been thinking about what you said and if there was one person who was capable of this it would be Ash."

"Really?"

"Yes, well, maybe not. I could be jumping to conclusions. I mean, Ash hasn't done anything really bad. He gives me a little bit of the creeps sometimes but I'm probably judging him a bit harshly." I was starting to confuse myself.

Travis laughed. "You almost did it. You almost started to believe that your client could have done this and then you just jumped right back. I almost got whiplash watching that little exercise."

"I'm glad I amused you," I muttered.

"Every day that I see you," said Travis. "Is there anything else that happened that morning that seemed to be out of place?"

I shook my head.

"If there is, I need you to tell me immediately. If any of the guys start acting in a way that you think is out of the ordinary, I want you to tell me, even if you think it doesn't mean anything. We need to know who did this. Ramos at least deserves that much."

I nodded.

Travis gave Griffin a searching look and, satisfied with what he saw there, he turned away and headed towards the mansion. I turned back around and looked out across the lake.

Griffin put an arm around my shoulder and pulled me into his side. "You okay?" he asked quietly.

I smiled tightly. "I'm always okay."

"Don't," Griffin said. "I know you have to put on a front for your clients and the people you work with. But not me. I am the one person in this world that you are completely safe with. Always know that. You can tell me anything, how you're feeling, what you need. I am here for you. You need to remember that."

"I know," I said simply.

"Enough to stop freaking out over the fact that I'm here?" Griffin teased.

"Not even close," I smiled.

"I'll try not to be too big a problem."

"I'm sure you will," I said. "I'd better get back to the house. The band should be getting up soon and I'll need to be on hand for whatever it is that they require. They're not the patient type."

"Have you ever had a client that was the patient type?" Griffin asked wryly.

The man had a point.

Chapter Fifteen

As Griffin and I walked up to the mansion, Jorge came out to meet us. "I'm going to need to steal your boyfriend for a while."

"What's happening?" I asked.

"There are some concerns about how Jolena got onto the property. The security staff who were at the front gate that night insist that there was no way she came through them. That means there has to be another point of entry and nobody seems to know what that could be. As the lawyer doesn't want the cop anywhere near the band we've been elected to search the perimeter of the property."

Griffin's expression was worried as he glanced down at me.

"You can't be by my side the whole time," I said firmly. "You need to do your job. If there's a problem I'll call for you."

"Make sure you do."

As I entered the mansion I could hear the first signs of the guys moving around. Walking into the kitchen, I found Dion and Sewell staring blearily at their coffee.

"You guys doing okay?"

I was rewarded with the standard grunts and nods.

"If you need anything just let me know."

Once again I got some grunts. It sounded like the guys were dealing with some major after party hangovers. I found Tim at his computer like I did every morning. He seemed to be in better condition than Dion and Sewell but then he always was. He may have been living the rock and roll lifestyle but Tim always had his eye on the prize. He was determined to be a billionaire in as short a time as possible and if anybody could do it, it was Tim. I admired the level of his ambition.

I found Ash already in the studio. In addition to being the lead singer of Crispy Spider, Ash was also the main songwriter for the band. When he wasn't partying he could usually be found writing lyrics or putting together music scores. I stood in the doorway while he was singing some lines to himself. I may not be overly fond of Ash but I could see why I was clearly in the minority. The man had a voice on him which could reach all the way into your soul. Ash held the last note and then looked up at me. I could feel myself being spellbound by the combination of his voice and those piercing eyes. He didn't look away as he put down his guitar and walked over to me.

"Can I help you, Trudie?" he asked quietly while standing closer to me than I was completely comfortable with.

I shook my head vigorously. "Just checking in on you to see if there was anything you needed me to do."

Ash smiled widely. "Anything?"

I almost rolled my eyes. I thought the time of these innuendos was past, but obviously Ash was bored and I was the only target available.

I stepped back. "You know what I mean, Ash."

"I've got some idea of what you mean but I'm a bit interested in exploring what I mean."

"Well, that is a pity," I said firmly. "I'm not interested in following up on whatever it is you are talking about. I don't know what's going on with you today, Ash, but I really need you to take it down a notch and move away."

Ash smiled, seemingly amused by my standard back off speech which usually came before a swift knee to the groin, if I felt it was absolutely necessary.

"Did you know that Vale is very upset that your boyfriend is working here? Do you by any chance know why that is?"

"He probably doesn't like the fact that there is now a cop within screaming distance," I said, hoping he would be able to take a hint.

"I don't think that's it. I think Vale may have just taken a liking to you and he doesn't like the competition being around. He doesn't seem to realize that it isn't your boyfriend he has to worry about."

"Trust me," I said. "If that's the case, he really does need to be worried about Griffin."

Ash reached out and stroked a finger down my cheek. "You always seem so controlled. Haven't you ever wanted to go a little wild?"

I shook my head. In the year I'd worked in Hollywood, I'd seen wild. It rarely ended well.

Ash leaned closer. "I think behind all those sensible clothes there is really a passionate woman just dying to get out. If you gave us a chance I could take you places you've never been before."

I had to stop myself from groaning in frustration. I loved working for narcissists who believed that nobody in the world could compare to them.

"I'm really not interested. My boyfriend provides me with more than enough excitement, thank you very much." I stepped back again, only to have Ash follow me.

"Are you sure?" he whispered.

I nodded as I wondered what was causing this weird mood. I hadn't felt exactly comfortable around Ash but he had never gone out of his way to seriously creep me out. I mentally ran through my options, ranging from gentle persuasion to the aforementioned knee to the groin. I had almost settled on the stomping on the instep of his foot while punching him in the throat maneuver that Griffin had taught me once when I'd mentioned dealing with guys like this. Admittedly, it may have been an overreaction but I was really not happy about how close Ash was and he seemed to be having a problem with the meaning of the word no. I almost cheered when I looked over Ash's shoulder and saw Vale enter the room. It didn't take him long to evaluate the situation.

Vale grabbed Ash's shoulder and swung him around.

"Leave her alone. She's not interested in your games."

Ash smiled cruelly. "She might be. Wouldn't be the first time a woman you wanted passed you over for me."

Vale flushed an angry red and swung wildly at Ash. Obviously Ash hadn't expected the blow because he looked stunned when it connected with his face.

I was almost as shocked as Ash. Despite his reputation, I had never seen Vale get violent with anyone.

Ash touched his jaw. "Was not expecting that. It seems I touched a nerve. I always knew you had a temper."

Vale stood stiffly with his fists clenched. "You need to back off now, Ash."

Ash cocked his head to one side, still stroking his jaw. "I'm afraid that is not going to happen," he said before dropping his head and rushing at Vale.

The two of them crashed to the floor. While they were distracted with pounding each other senseless I ran to the door.

"I need help," I yelled out, hoping that someone, preferably Jorge, was close by.

Instead I had Travis pounding up the stairs, followed by Detectives Fletchall and Pickett. The three of them stopped and surveyed the room. Vale and Ash were now rolling around on the floor, desperately hitting each other. While Fletchall and Pickett tried to separate the two combatants, Travis came over to me and put a hand on my shoulder.

"Are you okay, Trudie?" he asked quietly.

"Yes," I said shortly.

"What happened?"

"Ash was being an idiot and Vale reacted by being even more of an idiot."

Travis looked at me strangely. I didn't know why. To me that sounded like a succinct and accurate representation of the last ten minutes. Neither of the two men were covering themselves in glory. Vale had the opportunity to defuse the situation and he went for a punch to Ash's face. Despite my own violent thoughts when it came to dealing with Ash, I still thought it was an overreaction.

Fletchall and Pickett finally managed to pull the two men apart. Ash and Vale glared at each other. I had a feeling that the chances of them getting any work done today had just gone down the toilet. I really hoped that I was not going to get blamed for that.

"I'm going to need to speak to you, Trudie," Fletchall huffed out as he was holding Vale back from taking another swing at Ash.

"I think I'll be the one to interview Miss Eyre this time," said Pickett quietly as he seemed to be expending far less effort in controlling Ash. Although that could have more to do with the fact that with Ash's short attention span, he had already grown bored with the situation.

Fletchall scowled at his partner but seemed to acquiesce.

"Are we done here?" he growled at Ash and Vale.

Vale nodded sullenly, unsuccessfully trying to shrug off Fletchall's hand on his shoulder.

"I think we have an understanding of where we all stand now," Ash smiled in my direction.

Travis stiffened next to me and put an arm protectively around my shoulder. Of course, that was the moment that Griffin and Jorge finally turned up. I could see Griffin's eyes narrowing as he took in the scene before him.

"Aah, Trudie," Jorge said slowly. "What is going on here?"

"Your clients decided that having a brawl was a good way to start the day," Fletchall said. "I'm going to need to speak to them." Fletchall squinted at Griffin as if just noticing him. "Griffin, what the hell are you doing here?"

"Working," said Griffin, his eyes never leaving mine.

"I thought you were on holiday." Fletchall emphasized the word holiday and I'm sure he would have done air quotes with his fingers if he wasn't still keeping a tight grip on Vale.

"I am. I'm working a second job as security here."

The two detectives stared at Griffin incredulously. It seems I wasn't the only one having trouble believing the current turn of events.

"Really?" questioned Pickett.

I could understand the look of confusion on his face.

"Really," answered Griffin.

"Take these two downstairs and keep them separate." Pickett pushed Ash towards Jorge who did not seem thrilled at the current turn of events.

Fletchall led the group out of the room. Travis pulled his arm away and followed them out. That left Pickett, Griffin and me standing there, silently.

"Do you want to give us a bit of space, Detective Griffin," Pickett bit out.

Griffin looked in my direction and raised an eyebrow. "What do you want me to do, boss?"

"I'll be fine," I said. "I'll come down in a little bit."

He turned and left me alone with Detective Pickett who had a decidedly less friendly demeanor than Detective Fletchall. I had a feeling I was going back to interviews that were not enjoyable. Pickett took a seat and motioned to a couch across from him. I sat down gently and clasped my hands in my lap.

Pickett cleared his throat. "I'm hearing a lot about you, Miss Eyre."

That was probably not a good thing.

"According to my colleagues, you have a tendency to attract troublesome situations."

I inclined my head. It wasn't like I could argue with that statement.

"Your boyfriend, despite being a very good detective, is currently on suspension."

"That is hardly my fault," I ground out.

According to Griffin, his suspension had more to do with his personality than it did with anything that I may have done. I was inclined to believe that assessment.

Pickett shrugged. "It might not have been your fault but you do seem to attract more than your fair share of drama. That was always going to have some effect on Detective Griffin's career."

I decided silence seemed to be the best way to deal with that accusation.

Pickett looked at me keenly. "So, did you want to tell me why you seemed to be in the middle of a brawl today?"

"I came in to ask Ash whether he needed my help with anything. He was in a strange mood and started acting kind of inappropriately."

"How do you mean, inappropriately?"

"Just inappropriate. He was standing too close, trying to talk me into having some fun with him. I don't know, it all happened really fast and I was taken by surprise. Ash hasn't acted like that around me for a while. Vale came in and saw what was happening. He and Ash exchanged words and then the punches started flying."

"What kind of words?" Pickett looked interested.

I shrugged. "I don't know. Something about women choosing Ash instead of Vale. I didn't really know that they competed for women in that way."

"Have you ever seen them fight over women before?"

I shook my head. "To be perfectly honest, there are always so many women around when they are partying that there really isn't a need."

"Do you think this could have anything to do with Jolena Aaron?"

"I don't think so," I said slowly. "As far as I know, Jolena was only here for that one night. I wouldn't think that would be enough time for them to start a rivalry over her."

"You'd be surprised how quickly some women make an impression. Do you think Ash is capable of killing Jolena Aaron?"

I was surprised at the change in topic and hesitated.

Killing someone like Jolena had been killed would require passion. Ash had never, as long as I'd known him, shown any passion for anything besides his music. Despite the fact I seemed to want to find Ash responsible for Jolena's death, I just didn't seem to be able to convince myself.

"I think Ash is capable of killing her," I said slowly, trying very hard to choose my words carefully. "I'm just not sure whether he did kill her."

Pickett looked at me keenly and I started to feel uncomfortable. I had been right. This was in no way one of my better interviews. Even with Griffin I had been able to fall back on annoyance and anger. I couldn't quite work out what it was Detective Pickett wanted from me.

"How well do you know Detective Ramos?" he asked suddenly.

I shrugged cautiously. "She's Griffin's partner. I've usually only had dealings with her on a professional basis. The barbecue the other night was the first time I'd been in a social situation with her."

"How do you find her, when you've dealt with her?"

"She's always been strong, capable and professional. I have always known that she was a good cop. We may not have got along personally but I knew she had Griffin's back so that was all that I really cared about."

Pickett smiled in what I'm pretty sure he thought was an ingratiating way. It wasn't.

"I'm new to the precinct so I don't know her at all. I think that's one of the reasons I was assigned this case. It just seems strange that you find out that her girlfriend is cheating on her and then the girlfriend ends up dead."

"Sometimes coincidences happen," I said quietly.

"And sometimes they are not coincidences," Pickett said firmly.

"If you are looking at Ramos for Jolena's murder, then you are looking in the wrong place. Ramos and I may never have been best friends but I would stake my life on her not doing this."

"That's very loyal and brave of you but I've been in this job long enough to know that everyone is capable of doing the wrong thing when emotions are involved. Sometimes people make a quick decision and they can't step back from that. Good people make mistakes every day."

I knew good people made mistakes but I still could not believe that Ramos could do something like this.

"Is there anything else you think would assist me in my investigation?" Pickett asked.

I shook my head.

Pickett pulled a card out of his jacket and handed it to me. "If you need to speak to me at any time, just give me a call."

I nodded quietly and stood up.

"Trudie," Pickett's voice stopped me as I walked towards the door.

I turned around.

"You were nice to my wife at the barbecue the other day. She was very nervous about meeting all those new people and you made it a little easier for her. I've heard about other cases you have been involved in. I would hate to have to tell Dana that you had got hurt or worse. Be careful. Sometimes people aren't who you think they are. You should really be more wary when deciding who to put your faith into."

Chapter Sixteen

When I left the room I was not surprised to find that Griffin was waiting for me. He glared at Pickett as he walked past.

"Are you okay?" he asked.

"Yes, just been a bit of a strange morning."

"What the hell happened? You were supposed to be safe while Jorge and I were checking the perimeter."

"I was, well for most of it. I just did the same thing I do every morning. I checked to make sure the guys had everything they needed but then Ash went weird on me."

"What did he do?" Griffin lowered his voice.

"He thinks the same thing you do, that Vale likes me. Unfortunately he took that as a challenge. I think he was just trying to upset Vale by coming on to me."

"Do none of these people realize that you have a boyfriend?"

"Oh, they know. They just don't care."

I probably should have realized that telling my boyfriend some guy was trying to make another guy jealous by seducing me was not the best way to explain the situation.

"I really wish that you would find yourself a different job," Griffin said for what seemed like the millionth time.

"If I did that we wouldn't have these precious moments together."

Strangely enough, Griffin didn't seem to appreciate my observation.

"What the hell, Trudie?"

I turned around to find that Travis had decided to return and put his opinion forward.

"What?"

"You get left alone for all of half an hour and two of

the band end up brawling over you. They're still at each other's throats. What did you do?"

"Do not for a moment try to lay the blame for this on me. Something is going on between Vale and Ash and they're just using me as a convenient arguing point," I said indignantly.

"Why does it always have to be you?"

"How about the fact that I am the only female on the premises? Put Jorge in a dress and he might have been the one they were fighting over."

Travis and Griffin looked at me as I realized what I had just said.

Griffin cleared his throat. "Do you think of Jorge in a dress very often?"

"Okay, bad example."

"No, no," said Travis. "It just gave us an interesting view into what goes on in that mind of yours. We'll be filling Jorge in on it when we see him."

Great, I was never going to hear the end of that one. Of course Jorge chose that moment to join our little group.

"Hey, what's going on?"

"Oh nothing," interjected Travis before I could answer. "We've just discovered that Trudie has fantasies about you in a dress."

"Okay," said Jorge slowly. "We will definitely be talking about that later but for now we have to clear out."

"Why? We haven't been here that long," I queried.

"Now that the cops have calmed down the situation between Vale and Ash - nice going there, Trudie, by the way - they are executing a search warrant. All staff are requested to leave immediately."

"Why are they executing a search warrant?" Griffin asked.

"I don't know. You might want to ask your cop buddies about that one because they don't seem to be too interested in sharing information with the rest of us."

Jorge sounded exasperated. I could understand why. For a person who worked in security this was beginning to be an exercise in frustration. Before Jolena's death this job had been routine, or as routine as working security for a rock band could be. Now, we seemed to be all over the place.

"Do we have any idea when management are going to want us back?" I asked.

Jorge shook his head. "The cops have brought a pretty significant team with them. From the looks of it, they seem determined to tear this place apart."

"That's unusual," Griffin noted. "Budgets these days generally don't allow for a big team for a search warrant."

Jorge shrugged. "I've spoken to Monique and she has just said we need to stand down until we're called on again."

"That's it then." I turned to Travis. "Looks like you're on your own."

"That's nothing new," Travis grinned at me.

"Once again, you say the saddest things."

"You have got the softest heart of anyone I know," Travis smiled at me warmly.

Griffin put an arm around my shoulders and glared at Travis.

"Don't panic," drawled Travis. "I think one brawl over Trudie is enough for today. I'm not interested in starting a second one."

"Seriously, cupcake," Jorge said tiredly. "You are a trouble maker. Next time Monique calls me for a job with you, I'm going to start requesting hazard pay."

Chapter Seventeen

Dropping onto my couch, I waited for Griffin who I knew had followed me from the mansion.

"Want a coffee?" he asked as he walked through the door.

"In the worst possible way."

After making my coffee Griffin sat down on the couch beside me and I gratefully took the cup.

"So, you want to tell me exactly what happened this morning," he asked.

"Not particularly."

"Tell me," he insisted.

I sighed. "I went in to check on Ash to see if there was anything he needed. He was singing so I waited. When he finished I asked him if he wanted anything. He started going into schoolboy innuendo territory. I told him to stop it and that I wasn't interested. It seems Vale isn't happy about having you at the mansion. Ash then said that what Vale didn't understand was that Ash was the competition, not you."

"What happened next?"

"Vale came in and saw what Ash was doing. He told him to knock it off and then Vale punched Ash and it was on."

Griffin looked at me thoughtfully. "Did Ash say anything that could have set Vale off?"

I thought back. "Ash said something about it not being the first time that a woman had preferred him to Vale."

"Do you know what he was talking about?"

I shook my head. "No, I mean, there are so many women that come through. And Ash does seem to attract most of them. A lot of women, if given a choice, seem to go for the bad boy lead singer over the others. But it isn't as if the other guys are hurting in that area. There are more than enough groupies to go around."

"And yet they seemed to have focused their attention on you."

"I didn't do anything to encourage it," I said softly.

"I know," Griffin said tiredly. "I'm just having trouble with the fact that no matter what I do I can't seem to keep you safe. I honestly thought my being there would help but the first time you were out of my sight, this happens."

He looked so disheartened that I put down my coffee and wrapped my arms around him. "You can't be with me every moment of the day. You just need to believe that I will not do anything stupid. I don't think I was in any real danger this morning. It was just an uncomfortable situation. Unfortunately, in my work, uncomfortable situations seem to be common."

"This thing with Vale and Ash, is it going to be a problem when you go back to work?" Griffin asked as he stroked his hand up and down my back.

"It could be, I don't know. It wasn't an issue I was expecting to have to deal with. I'm sure Jorge has filled Monique in on what the problem is and I'm expecting a call from her at some point. We'll discuss it and if it looks like it will get in the way of me doing my job, I'll step aside and one of the other personal assistant's will take my place."

"Is that a problem for you?" Griffin said. "Your job doesn't seem that secure. How will you do financially? I can help you if you want."

It was sweet that he was worried.

"Monique has a waiting list of placements that she can put me into. I know it seems that all my assignments are difficult but that's only because I have a higher level of tolerance for self-important clients. As a result I generally get the worst ones. Every now and then Monique will give me a less difficult job if I request it."

"Good."

We sat there quietly for a while, just enjoying the comfort of being together. I felt protected and safe in the circle of Griffin's arms and I couldn't imagine myself wanting to be anywhere else. This was why Ash's offer of being wild didn't interest me.

"So, did you and Jorge find anything while I was having my drama in the house?"

Griffin nodded. "We found that there are plenty of access points to the grounds that hadn't been found before. There is a gate down behind the lake. It looks secure if you just give it a cursory inspection, which it seems is all anyone has ever done. The padlock on it looks locked but you can pull it apart relatively easily. That's one point. There are also some trees that overhang the wall that someone could climb and then drop down into the grounds. To be perfectly honest, there are so many ways to get onto that property that it is almost useless to have security at the front gate."

"How about security cameras?"

"Another area where they are woefully inadequate. There are some cameras but they don't even come close to covering the whole grounds. You could almost march an army into that place and security would miss it. Travis has a huge job on his hands if he wants to fix that mess. Then you add in the very real possibility that Jolena's death could have been an inside job and your problem list goes through the roof."

"Travis isn't really there for security evaluation," I said.

"I didn't think he was," replied Griffin. "I know how this town works, remember. I'm betting the record company hired him to find out who killed Jolena so they can preempt any bad publicity that could come the band's way."

"Got it in one."

"Maybe he'll have more luck than Fletchall and Pickett," Griffin said thoughtfully. "The band and their management will probably be a bit more forthcoming with him. He could get the jump on them."

"He told me that he will pass along the information. He isn't going to let them cover anything up."

I could feel some of the tenseness in Griffin start to ease.

"That's good to know. Ramos is really going to need to get some answers."

I was distracted when my phone started ringing.

"That will be Monique," I said as I searched through my bag.

"Hello, Monique," I said when I finally managed to get hold of it. "How are you this fine day?"

I grinned at Griffin as he shook his head.

"I'm hearing stories, ma petite. Stories that are causing me some concern."

"Has Jorge been telling tales?"

"Our security contingent is becoming alarmed that the situation you are in may be becoming volatile."

Monique always phrased things so nicely.

"I'm fine, Monique. This morning was just a little glitch. I don't think that the guys are coping well with the situation and they are acting out in some weird ways."

"They need to stop acting out around you."

There was an edge to Monique's voice that I hadn't heard before. I had a feeling that arguing with her was not the way to go today. She had obviously reached the end of her patience when it came to this situation. I decided not to make this hard for her.

"What do you want me to do, Monique?" I asked quietly.

Griffin raised an eyebrow. Obviously my not arguing the point was a new concept for him. I hoped he enjoyed the show because he had very little chance of seeing me employ this technique with him.

Monique sighed. "What I want is for you to be as far away from that property as is humanly possible. I want you to never have any contact with any of those people again.

Unfortunately, the client is adamant that you are to stay. It seems that despite the issues that your recent run in with Ash has caused, you have been more effective with keeping the band on track than anyone else they have previously had in their employ."

Monique sounded truly irritated that I was doing the job that I was paid for.

"So, what do you want me to do?"

"I want you to view every interaction with these people with suspicion. I do not want you to take any chances. I want Jorge and that man of yours to know at every moment exactly what you are doing."

"Do you also want to have a GPS tracking device implanted in me," I said, with just a small amount of sarcasm.

"If I thought I could get away with it, I would," Monique retorted. "I know you say that you are careful but I have a very bad feeling that this situation is spiraling out of control."

I remained silent as I let her get the frustration out of her system.

"Stay close to the people who want to protect you. Be aware of what is going on around you at all times. Now is not the moment to do anything stupid."

"I don't do stupid," I retorted, feeling a little like I was being reprimanded by a teacher.

Monique sighed heavily. "I know you don't. I just want to make sure that you are safe. The next job you get is going to be easy, where the worst risk to you is getting a paper cut."

I had no problem with that. I figured I was due an easy job.

"Be careful and call me if you want out. Management have indicated that they believe the police will be finished by this evening. They want staff back on board early tomorrow to clean up the mess the police made. The band is currently in a hotel. They will be returning late tomorrow afternoon after the staff have finished their job. I do not want you to be left alone with anyone. At all times you will have Jorge or that man of yours glued to your side."

"I can't do my job like that," I protested.

"I don't care," Monique said firmly. "That is my condition for you continuing to do this job."

I could tell that she had reached the point where arguing was a fruitless exercise.

"Yes, ma'am," I said, feeling a little rebellious.

"Good." Monique finally sounded like she had found some peace with the situation.

As I got off the phone I turned to Griffin who was watching me carefully.

"That sounded like fun."

"Monique is not dealing well with me at the moment," I said. "I have a feeling that she is going to take me off this job at the first opportunity."

I saw Griffin's smile.

"Now is not the time to enjoy the moment," I warned. "I understand everyone's concern but all this second guessing and protectiveness is starting to get on my nerves. I have to be able to do my job."

"I understand your frustration and I will endeavor not to add to it," Griffin said solemnly.

"Oh, honey. I don't know what conflict resolution course taught you that line but you need to work a lot harder on it. You try that on me again and we are going to have words because there was no sincerity there at all."

Griffin at least had the good grace to look sheepish.

"Okay, I agree with everything Monique is obviously saying and I really wish I could say that I would stop being overly protective but that is not going to happen."

I really wanted to argue but I knew that was the best I was going to get out of him. If Jorge had been standing there, I wouldn't have got any better.

A knock on the door interrupted the glare I was

shooting in Griffin's direction.

I opened it and was surprised to find Crystal standing there, chewing her lip.

"What's wrong?" I said, instantly on alert. It took a lot for Crystal to look that nervous.

"I need you to come to my mother's bachelorette party."

That was unexpected.

"Why?"

"Okay," Crystal said in that rushed way she has when she is not really sure where she stands on an issue. "The fact that my mother has been married so many times meant that I wasn't really expecting that she'd want a bachelorette party. I just naturally assumed that the term bachelorette no longer applied to you when your weddings headed into double figures."

I could see where that was a logical assumption to make.

"The thing is, Roxy wanted to do something where she and I could bond with John's daughters."

"And she thought a bachelorette party was the way to go?"

Crystal shrugged helplessly. "What can I say? She may be acting differently these days but she's still Roxy."

"So, why am I supposed to come along?"

"I'm using you as social protection. I'm hoping that with you there it won't be quite as excruciatingly uncomfortable as I think it is going to be."

"That sounds like fun."

"I'll owe you," Crystal said.

"That goes without saying."

"Miss Betsy organized the afternoon so she'll be there to keep us company."

"What do you mean, Miss Betsy organized the bachelorette party?"

Crystal smiled guiltily. "I panicked. I didn't know what to do and Miss Betsy said she'd take care of it for me."

"Did you by any chance give her any guidance or did you just ask her to organize something?"

"Remember how I said I panicked. Well, I really did, and I had to get to work. Miss Betsy was right there and she said that it would be no problem at all for her to create a day that Roxy would never forget."

I had a feeling that none of us were going to forget it. Griffin, who had been watching the conversation with avid interest, had a faintly disturbed expression on his face.

"Have you by any chance asked her what she has organized?" he asked.

Crystal turned to him. "After I thought about it, I called her up to give her some rules, but she was so excited that I didn't have the heart to rain on her parade."

"That's going to be interesting," Griffin murmured.

I took a deep breath. "Maybe we're overreacting. Miss Betsy would realize how important this is to you. I'm sure she hasn't planned anything too outrageous."

Neither Griffin nor Crystal seemed to be too convinced by my argument. To be perfectly honest, neither was I. Thanks to Miss Betsy, I now had a working knowledge of how to pick most locks and break into a car. These were skills that I had never realized that I might need until Miss Betsy got bored one day and convinced me that every modern woman should have them. I still hadn't been game enough to tell Griffin about that day. Seems life in Hollywood as a stunt woman had provided Miss Betsy with a set of life skills which couldn't be matched. She also seemed to be determined to share those life skills with the tenants at the apartment building that she owned.

"When are we going?" I asked.

"Pretty much now," Crystal smiled apologetically.

"Give me five minutes so I can get myself sorted out and I'll meet you in the parking lot."

Crystal nodded and walked out.

I almost ran to the bedroom and started looking for something appropriate to wear.

"Do I need to be worried?"

Griffin had followed me and leaned against the door frame as I started throwing clothes off.

"Probably," I said. "I have no idea what I'm doing or how long I'm going to be. All I know is that the rest of my day is now resting in the slightly unhinged hands of Miss Betsy."

"How bad could it be?"

I contemplated for a moment telling Griffin about the fact that I could now break into a car or one of the apartments with very little effort thanks to Miss Betsy. At the end of that moment I realized what a stupid idea that was. Did he really need to be even more worried about me than he already was? I consoled myself thinking that I was only protecting him.

"Maybe not too bad," I said.

I kept reminding myself of that as I drove my car with Crystal sitting beside me and Miss Betsy giving directions.

Chapter Eighteen

Standing outside the building Miss Betsy had directed us to, I didn't know whether to be concerned or relieved. When Crystal had told me that Miss Betsy was organizing our activities for the day, I had to admit, there was a small part of me which had been worried that I might not get through the day without jumping out of a plane. I would not have put it past Miss Betsy to use this opportunity to convince Crystal and I that skydiving was another skill that every modern woman should have. So, from that point of view, I was relieved that it seemed that my feet would be staying on firm ground. The concerned part of this situation came in when I realized that we would be spending our afternoon at a gun range.

"This is awesome."

Obviously Crystal did not seem to have the same concerns that I did regarding the suitability of going to a gun range for a bachelorette party.

Miss Betsy bumped me with her shoulder. "I told you that I was going to teach you how to shoot at some point."

I had forgotten about that, possibly on purpose.

I smiled weakly. "Should be fun."

"Here comes Roxy," Crystal said quietly.

I looked up and watched the way Roxy walked down the street. Even from this distance I could see she looked nervous. She was followed by two very tall, younger women who didn't look any happier to be here than she did.

I lowered my head and spoke to Crystal. "Aren't John's daughters happy about this marriage?"

"Doesn't look like it, does it?" said Crystal.

"Maybe choosing a gun range wasn't such a good idea," interjected Miss Betsy. "Those girls look like they would quite happily pitch your mother out into the middle of traffic."

"To be perfectly honest," said Crystal, "if someone with Roxy's past was involved with my dad, I'd be losing it completely. It isn't as if she is prime wife material."

If you looked at it objectively, she wasn't. Roxy had the staying power of a wet paper towel. She might be claiming true love now but her past gave a very different picture. This was a woman who fell in and out of love very easily. I didn't blame John's daughters for looking the way they did. The strained smile on Roxy's face as she walked up to us showed that she was also very much aware that John's daughters didn't approve of her.

"Crystal, Trudie. It's so good to see you both here. These are John's daughters. Megan and Sally, this is my daughter Crystal and her friend Trudie."

Megan and Sally nodded at us.

"This is Miss Betsy," Crystal indicated to the older woman while smiling brightly. "She organized our day today so I'm sure we're all going to have heaps of fun."

I thought that was very nicely done. In one swift move Crystal had passed all responsibility for the day onto Miss Betsy. Miss Betsy didn't seem to have any problem with that. She clapped her hands together.

"Now we are going to have some fun today. Our first step is learning how to shoot a gun, the correct way. Every woman should know how to protect herself, No point in waiting for Prince Charming to rescue you because he doesn't exist."

Crystal and I exchanged glances. That was an interesting theme to take into a bachelorette party. We shouldn't have been surprised though. Miss Betsy was very much a supporter of the theory that a woman could only depend on herself. Megan and Sally were exchanging worried glances. Roxy seemed to have a perpetual frown marring her perfectly smooth face. I could see there was a part of her that regretted suggesting that a bachelorette party was a good idea. I could also see that Megan and Sally had already decided that they were not going to enjoy today.

Upon entering the gun range I was not surprised when Miss Betsy greeted the man behind the counter as if they were old friends.

"Miss Betsy," he smiled as he held out his hands and gripped hers.

"Billy," Miss Betsy said warmly.

She looked over her shoulder at the rest of the group.

"This is Billy. He owns this place and he is going to help us today."

Billy grinned widely at us. "Good to see you here today, ladies. Do any of you have any experience with guns?"

I was not surprised when Crystal put up her hand. I knew she'd had a bit of a wild past when she was younger. Megan and Sally exchanged glances and shook their heads. I already knew about Miss Betsy's experience. Roxy had been watching Megan and Sally closely and she shook her head as well. I wasn't really sure how confident I was that she was telling the truth. I had a feeling that she was very much aware that John's daughters were not too keen on this marriage. I wouldn't put it past her to downplay things just to fit in with them. I reluctantly put up my hand and watched Crystal's eyes widen in shock.

"You've shot a gun?"

"Yes."

"But you hate guns."

"I will admit I'm not overly fond of them."

"How do I not know this about you? You're my best friend. I'm supposed to know everything about you."

Crystal seemed to be a little upset. I tried to head her off before she worked herself into a real state.

"My dad taught me how to shoot a rifle. Once, when I was twelve. I grew up on a farm where there was a possibility that I would have to deal with injured animals. Dad thought it was important that I learned how to use a weapon properly. I never did but I roughly know my way around a rifle, enough to use it in an emergency situation."

"Ever use a handgun?" Billy asked.

I shook my head. "No, and to be perfectly honest my one and only lesson with the rifle was over ten years ago, so I'm pretty much a novice."

"That's fine," said Billy. "I'll take you through the basics. You'll do great."

I could see he was trying to project a confident demeanor but I could also see that he was noticing the less than pleasant looks that Megan and Sally were shooting in Roxy's direction. Crystal had moved closer to her mother in a defensive stance. Billy glanced at Miss Betsy who smiled encouragingly. I had a feeling Billy was beginning to regret taking this booking, regardless of how fond he was of Miss Betsy. He hesitated for a moment before shepherding us into the range.

"Well, Ladies," Billy clapped his hands together, speaking loudly as if trying to inject some enthusiasm into the group. "There are four rules in my gun range." He pointed to a line on the floor. "Number one rule is that you never cross that line without my direct say so. Number two rule is that you never, ever point a weapon in the direction of another person. Number three rule is that you do not point the muzzle of a loaded weapon lower than that target over there."

"Why not?" interrupted Megan.

"Ladies, could you please look up."

We all looked up at the ceiling to see holes with pen marks around them.

"See those holes up there. That is what happens when rule number three is not obeyed. You point the muzzle of the gun too low and accidentally shoot the floor. I am now going to introduce you to a concept called ricochet. A bullet hits the ground and it can bounce anywhere. The best case in this situation is that you add to my collection of holes in the ceiling. Worst case scenario is that you hit one of your group or, more importantly, me. That is not going to happen so I want you to remember rule number three like it was printed on your brain." Billy glared at us all meaningfully. "Rule number four is that you never have your finger on the trigger until the moment you mean to shoot the gun. You are not in a war zone where reflexes are important and every second counts. You can take your sweet time with aiming and squeezing off each shot. I do not want to see fingers on triggers until the moment you take your shot."

After a cursory look over our group Billy chose me to begin the demonstration. I doubted it was because he could see my inherent sharp shooting abilities. I think it was more to do with the fact that I looked to be the calmest person in this part of the range. He placed the handgun on the counter in front of me and I gently picked it up. I wrapped my hand around the grip. It felt surprisingly more comfortable than I had thought it was going to.

"Now, I need you to point the gun at the target and line it up," he said from behind me.

I brought the gun up and did my best to aim it. I could feel my arm shaking a little. Whether it was from the unfamiliar weight of the gun or from nerves, I wasn't sure.

"When you feel that you've got it aimed, squeeze the trigger."

I took in a quick breath, held it and fired the gun. I felt the recoil up my arm and took a small step back.

"Not bad," said Billy as he retrieved the target.

It wasn't great either. At least I hadn't missed the target completely but you could tell that there was very little chance of me winning any sharp shooting competitions in the near future.

"It was a fine first effort," Miss Betsy praised, her enthusiasm a little over the top considering the actual placement of the bullet.

"Absolutely," said Crystal.

"Sure it was," Billy said, slightly less enthusiastically.

Before long Billy had us all lined up and was yelling encouragement. Megan and Sally seemed to be even more unsure about using the guns than I was. At least I was hitting the target on a reasonably regular basis.

Crystal and Miss Betsy were putting us all to shame and I could see Billy nodding appreciatively. I looked over at Roxy's target. For a woman claiming never to have used a gun, she seemed to be doing pretty well.

After a while I stepped back and grabbed a drink of water. I had to admit that when we had first arrived, I had doubted the wisdom of this exercise. Putting Roxy and her seemingly reluctant future stepdaughters in a gun range seemed to be what I would call a recipe for disaster but I could now see the wisdom behind it. Crystal and Miss Betsy had placed themselves between Megan and Sally, and Roxy, minimizing their contact and the potential for conflict. I swallowed some water as Billy collected my target.

"Not bad," he said grudgingly in what I'm assuming was him trying to be generous to a paying customer.

He passed over the target and I had a chance to look at it myself. 'Not bad' seemed to be the most accurate description. It wasn't particularly good either but it wasn't as if I was looking at taking it up competitively.

The door to the range opened and I looked over. I was surprised to see that Ramos had entered the gun range. Her features tightened when she spotted me, before deliberately turning and taking her place at one of the lanes.

Miss Betsy came up and stood beside me. "Isn't that your boyfriend's partner?"

I nodded.

"She doesn't look like she is too happy with you."

That was a bit of an understatement.

"Her girlfriend was murdered a couple of days ago at the place where I'm currently working."

"And she is blaming you for it somehow, isn't she?" Miss Betsy asked shrewdly.

"Yeah."

Miss Betsy looked over at Ramos again. "Whatever happened, you have to know that it wasn't your fault."

I hugged Miss Betsy impulsively. I loved her sense of loyalty. She had no knowledge of any of the facts regarding Jolena's death but she was still completely sure that I was not involved in any way at all.

"It doesn't matter what I know or what I think. She's grieving and I understand that. Griffin's helping her as much as possible and he's told me that she has a lot of good people around her. The best thing is for me to stay out of her way."

Miss Betsy looked thoughtful. "Maybe she just needs something to distract her for a little while."

I had a bad feeling that I knew where this was heading. Miss Betsy straightened her shoulders and walked over to Ramos.

Crystal came up behind me. "What's going on?"

"I don't know," I said slowly, "but I have a feeling that our little party is about to expand."

"God, I hope so," muttered Crystal. "This has got to be one of the most uncomfortable bachelorette parties I have ever been to. It looks like John's daughters hate Roxy."

That was patently obvious although considering how Ramos felt about me, I didn't know whether her addition to the group was going to help the dynamics.

Crystal lowered her voice. "I think they're going to try to stop the wedding."

I wasn't surprised. Those two women had that determined look in their eyes. They were ready to protect their father from whatever supposedly stupid move he was about to make. I wasn't saying that they were wrong. Roxy would definitely not be my first choice of life partner for my father. But the man was an adult, fully capable of making his own decisions. That's the thing about family though. They sometimes get so caught up in protecting those they love that they forget they can't bulldoze their way over other people's decisions without some fallout happening.

Miss Betsy finished her conversation with Ramos and came over to where Crystal and I were standing.

"She's coming with us to the club," she said triumphantly.

"Are you sure?" I asked.

"What club?" Crystal asked suspiciously.

Miss Betsy's eyes twinkled. That should have been my first clue.

"She's grieving at a gun range. That is not right and it is not healthy."

I wasn't really sure how dragging Ramos to a club could be considered healthy either.

"And in answer to your question, Crystal, we are going to a club that I go to with my gardening group for some drinks after being in here. Just to finish off the day."

Considering we were already in quite possibly the most miserable bachelorette party ever, how much worse could it get?

Chapter Nineteen

I had to revisit that question as we stood in the very out of the way club that Miss Betsy had brought us to. Megan, Sally and Ramos had identical expressions on their faces. None of them wanted to be here and they were making that very obvious to everyone around them.

"Miss Betsy," the bartender called out her name, waving us through.

Miss Betsy smiled and acknowledged several greetings from staff and patrons. Why did it not surprise me that the bar where everyone knew Miss Betsy's name was one which had shirtless male waiters?

"I'm not sure if this is such a good idea," Crystal whispered in my ear.

"I think we lost the choice when you asked Miss Betsy to organize this."

"Lesson learned," murmured Crystal.

"Bit late for Roxy though," I said. "She wanted a bonding experience with her new stepdaughters. I heard miserable circumstances can bring people closer together."

We looked at the four women who were now seated around a table, studiously ignoring each other and us.

"I don't think that's going to work tonight," Crystal said.

I hoped Miss Betsy wasn't feeling too badly about the way the day was panning out. I don't think she could have come up with anything that these women would have been happy with. They seemed determined not to enjoy themselves. I looked over to see Miss Betsy flirting outrageously with one of the waiters. Seemed she was okay with it.

For the next hour I counted the minutes until the world's worst bachelorette party could finish. I kept glancing in Ramos's direction. After I did that for the hundredth time, she sighed heavily.

"What, Trudie?"

"I just want to make sure you're okay," I said quietly.

"I'm stuck here trying to think of a polite way to extricate myself without hurting your friend's feelings, but other than that I'm fine."

I was surprised. I had assumed that Ramos wouldn't care that much about hurting Miss Betsy's feelings. Obviously Miss Betsy had endeared herself more to Ramos in a five minute conversation than I had managed to do in the year we had known each other.

Miss Betsy came over to the group. "Well, ladies, anyone interested in skydiving?"

That was one way to bring a bad bachelorette party to a screeching halt. Megan and Sally almost broke a speed record giving their excuses. Roxy smiled apologetically and followed the two women out of the club.

"How about you three?" Miss Betsy asked with a slightly fiendish look in her eyes.

"No," chorused Crystal and I. Unlike Ramos we had no compunction about saying no to Miss Betsy. We had known her too long and been involved in too many of her schemes to blindly follow her lead.

"I think I'm going home," announced Ramos.

"Maybe next time, dear," Miss Betsy said gently and I could actually see the steel exterior that Ramos presented to the world melt at the compassion in Miss Betsy's eyes.

"I'll think about it," she said. "It's been a while since I've been skydiving."

I wasn't surprised Ramos had already tackled the whole jumping out of an airplane thing. In direct contrast, the thought of doing it terrified me so much that I felt sick.

As we walked out of the bar, I noticed that Ramos had stopped and was rummaging through her bag.

"Do you need a ride home?" I asked her.

She shook her head. "No, I'm fine. I need to go back in

anyway. I think I left my phone at the bar. I must have taken it out when I was paying for a drink."

"I can help you look for it if you like."

"No, Trudie," she said firmly. "I'll be fine. I had it earlier so I know I only just put it down."

"Okay," I said awkwardly. What exactly did you say to someone who blamed you for wrecking their life?

Ramos sighed. "I'm fine, Trudie. Really. I just need some space to get my head back in the game."

I nodded sharply. "I'll see you later."

I walked over to where Miss Betsy was waiting for me. My eye was caught by a car that looked slightly familiar in the darkened corner of the parking lot.

Miss Betsy looked over to me. "Do you recognize that car?"

I should have known that she would be the one to pick up on my concerns.

"I think I remember seeing it at the gun range," I said thoughtfully.

"And now it's sitting outside a bar which isn't overly well known. It seems to be a bit of a coincidence, doesn't it?"

I nodded, glancing back to where Crystal had cornered Ramos who looked as if she was desperately trying to make her getaway.

"Is there a reason for any of us to be followed?" Miss Betsy lowered her voice as her brow furrowed.

"I have no idea," I replied.

"One way to find out."

I watched in horrified shock as Miss Betsy strode purposefully over to the car. The engine started up and the car sped off down the street. But not before I caught a glimpse of Marty Fletchall behind the wheel.

Miss Betsy stood resolutely in the middle of the parking lot, studying the fleeing car.

"Did you see him?" she asked.

I nodded.

"Any idea who it was?"

"He's a cop who is working the murder of Ramos's girlfriend."

"Do they think that poor, sweet girl had something to do with her girlfriend's death?"

I nodded. "There is a slight possibility that they are following up on."

Miss Betsy sighed. "People are so dumb sometimes. Anyone could tell that she would never do anything like that."

Miss Betsy had obviously decided to include Ramos in her circle of protectees.

"I'll talk to Griffin about it when I get home tonight. He might be able to follow up and see what the hell is going on."

I was beginning to feel annoyed and protective on Ramos's behalf. An emotion I was sure that she would be keen to discourage.

Crystal, having finally released Ramos from her social torture, walked up to us. "I've missed something, haven't I?"

"We don't know," said Miss Betsy. "Maybe. We need to check with Griffin first."

"Like that doesn't sound ominous," said Crystal.

The ride home was quiet as the three of us were lost in our thoughts.

Miss Betsy broke the silence. "Well, that was a truly unpleasant day."

"That it was," I agreed.

"It wasn't anything you did," Crystal was quick to assure her. "I didn't realize the level of animosity towards my mother from John's family."

Miss Betsy shrugged. "I'm not worried about it, sugar. Some people are just determined to be miserable. Wouldn't want to be in the groom's shoes at the moment though. I think they will be having some serious words before the wedding."

"You want to come and see the fireworks?" asked Crystal.

"Isn't it a little late for an invitation?" asked Miss Betsy.

"Unfortunately, it seems that a large proportion of the groom's side has decided to boycott the wedding. There are seats available for the show. You can bring one of the guys from the club as a date if you like."

I hated to hear the defeat in Crystal's voice.

"What's going on?" I asked gently.

Crystal turned to me. "I shouldn't care how this wedding goes. Roxy has completely ignored me my entire life and I'm caring about the fact that some guy's family is assuming that the ten time married ex-showgirl is a bad bet in the marriage stakes. I want to defend her even though I know that it is pretty much an impossible task. Why do I want to do that?"

"Because, despite many reasons not to be, you are a good, forgiving person."

Crystal slumped back in her seat. "That's just great."

Chapter Twenty

When I walked into my apartment I found Griffin in the living room.

He turned off the television. "You're home a lot earlier than I was expecting."

"It wasn't really the raucous night that most bachelorette parties are. We were a bit concerned that the stepdaughters-to-be would do some serious damage to Roxy if we kept it going until everyone got too drunk and started saying what they really thought about the situation."

"That good, huh?" Griffin said with a grimace as I sat next to him on the couch.

"I think they are just being protective of their dad. Roxy doesn't exactly inspire confidence when it comes to marital devotion. I'm guessing there have been many family discussions between those two women and their father regarding his choice of bride."

"But other than that, it was good?"

I frowned thoughtfully. "Good might be overstating it. Tense and uncomfortable might be more accurate. And it didn't improve when Ramos joined us at the gun range."

"You were at a gun range?" I could see Griffin smiling.

"Yes, I was."

"How did you do?"

"We established that shooting a handgun is not one of my talents but, fortunately, I will always have my winning personality to fall back on," I said dryly.

Griffin laughed.

"And after the gun range we went to the bar where Miss Betsy goes with her gardening club."

Griffin quirked an eyebrow. "I know how you work, Trudie. You said it that way because you are hoping that I will get the impression that it was a tame night out but you forget that I know Miss Betsy. Exactly what kind of bar was it?"

Foiled again.

"There were no strippers as such," I said in a rush.

"Oh, because that's a great way to explain a situation."

"It was just a bar where the waiters were shirtless. There was no touching or grinding or anything that could possibly be construed as inappropriate."

"Oh, well, that's good to know," Griffin said with just a touch less sarcasm than I was expecting. "Wait a minute. Are you saying that Ramos joined you?"

I nodded.

"Why on Earth would Ramos join Roxy's bachelorette party?"

"Miss Betsy saw her at the gun range and felt that wasn't a healthy way to deal with her grief."

"I agree with her there but I wouldn't have thought that joining you lot would have been a much better way to deal with her grief," Griffin said.

"Quite possibly true," I agreed. "But Miss Betsy was pretty determined and you know how that usually goes."

Ramos probably never stood a chance.

"How was she?" Griffin asked quietly.

"Surly, pissed off with the world."

"So, normal?"

"Pretty much," I agreed.

"Did she enjoy herself at all?"

I shook my head. "But in all fairness, I don't think anyone really enjoyed themselves today. I'm not really sure how the wedding is going to be tomorrow, or whether it even goes ahead. John's daughters really do not want him marrying Roxy."

"Guess we'll see tomorrow," Griffin said thoughtfully.

We sat quietly for a moment.

"Can you give me a good reason for Detective Fletchall sitting outside both the gun range and the club we went to?"

I could feel Griffin tensing beside me. "He may be following Ramos if he suspects she killed Jolena."

"He wasn't being very subtle about it. Both Miss Betsy and I spotted him. He drove off when Miss Betsy went to confront him."

Griffin groaned. "Why would she do that? Approaching a strange car that may be following you is not one of the smartest moves a person can make. She does know that, doesn't she?"

"Probably, but this is Miss Betsy we are talking about. I wouldn't put it past her to try to drag the guy out of his car if he hadn't driven off."

My phone rang and I reached over to grab it.

"Hello," I said, frowning at the unfamiliar number.

"Is this Trudie Eyre?" I tried to place the slightly familiar voice.

"Yes. Who is this?"

"It's Detective Desmond Pickett. I was wondering if you could come down to the precinct.

"Why?" I asked suspiciously.

Pickett sighed. I could tell he was one of those people who preferred it if you just accepted what they said blindly and didn't ask any questions. If that was the case, today was not going to be one of his lucky days.

"I would appreciate your assistance with some issues that have come to light regarding Jolena Aaron's death."

"Really?" I couldn't help the suspicion in my voice.

"Yes, a new line of inquiry has presented itself and I just wanted to go over your evidence again. Make sure we haven't missed anything."

"Now?"

"Yes, I would really appreciate it."

I could tell that had been painful for him. If I listened hard enough, I could hear him grinding his teeth. My experience with Detective Pickett gave the indication that he wasn't someone who would easily ask for help, especially not from a civilian.

"I'll come straight in," I said before turning off the phone.

"What's going on?" Griffin asked, instantly on alert.

"According to Detective Pickett they have a new lead and he wants me to come in and go over my evidence again.

Griffin frowned. "That sounds strange. Did he say why he wanted to see you in particular?"

I shook my head. "He didn't give any details. Just that he wanted to talk to me."

Griffin grabbed his keys. "I'll drive you in."

I hadn't expected anything else.

Chapter Twenty-One

Pickett was waiting for us at the precinct. He gave Griffin a cursory nod when he saw him behind me.

"Thank you for coming in, Trudie. If you'll just follow me to an interview room, we'll get this done as quickly as possible."

I left Griffin and followed Pickett towards the interrogation room that I had come to know so well.

At the doorway he turned and gestured me inside.

"Please take a seat. I'll be right in."

As I stepped through the door I was shocked to find Vale handcuffed to the table and was even more surprised when the door was closed firmly behind me. I suddenly had a very bad feeling.

"What's going on, Vale?" I asked nervously.

"Looks like they want you and I to have a little chat," Vale said humorlessly.

I had no problem with having a chat with Vale. I did have a problem with being put in a room with a man who was handcuffed to a table. To my limited understanding, that meant that someone thought he was dangerous. Most likely the police officer who put me in here.

I cleared my throat. "Seriously, Vale. I need you to tell me what's going on?"

Preferably before I started panicking.

"They think I killed Jolena."

I could feel my jaw drop. "They can't be serious."

Of all the ways that I had assumed this case would go, this wasn't one of them.

"That Detective who shoved you in here with me seems to be very serious. I wouldn't talk until my lawyer got here. Seems he thought you would be able to get the information out of me."

Detective Pickett and I were going to have some words. Serious words. Especially about the fact that he seemed to be fine with putting me in a room with a suspected murderer.

"I didn't do it."

Vale's protestation of innocence, while not unexpected for a man shackled to a table in a police precinct, did at least provide me with some small level of comfort.

"Why do they think you did?" I asked, trying to portray a calm attitude while staying as close to the door as I could.

"They found out that Jolena and I dated for a bit in high school. It was so long ago and it wasn't for very long but they're building it up as if she was the love of my life."

"Was she?" I asked, curious in spite of myself.

Vale shook his head emphatically.

"I had a few girlfriends in high school and I've had a lot more since then. I never even thought about Jolena until we ran into each other a couple of weeks ago at some promotional photo shoot I did. She jumped on the fact that I was now in a band and wanted to come to one of our parties. I wasn't really keen on it because, you know how those parties usually end up. I really wouldn't want any woman that I know going to one of them, but she insisted. I wasn't around when she got thrown out but they think I was jealous of Ash."

"Were you? I asked.

Vale shook his head again. "Jolena has been nothing more than a vague memory for a very long time. When I ran into her, I barely recognized her. She was the one who came up to me."

"The police must have something more on you than just the fact that you knew her," I said carefully.

Vale held my eyes. "When they did the search of the mansion they found a necklace that Jolena wore all the time in my room."

I was beginning to understand why he was handcuffed to a table. Something must have shown in my eyes.

"I didn't do it, Trudie. I need you to believe that."

There was a part of me that did believe him. I liked Vale. But if there was something the police I knew kept telling me, it was that even the best of people are capable of making a bad decision in the heat of emotion.

"Why am I here, Vale? Why do they think that I can get information out of you?"

Vale raised his eyes to mine. "They think that the fact that I hit Ash for putting moves on you puts you in the same position as Jolena."

That was a statement that was going to keep me up nights. No way did I want to think for a moment that I was in the same category as a murder victim.

My musings about an upcoming bout of insomnia were interrupted when the door was flung open and Griffin stood in the doorway, seething with anger. "We're done here. I'm taking you home, Trudie."

I didn't care what other people said about Griffin. The man had an exquisite sense of timing.

I nodded and started for the door.

"Trudie," Vale called out. "Can I ask one favor of you?"

I stopped and turned back.

"Could you feed Buddy in the morning? It doesn't look like my chances are good at getting out of here by then. I don't want him to suffer."

"I'll take care of him," I said softly and beat a hasty retreat. I wondered if it was possible for a murderer to care so much about a goat.

Outside the interrogation room, Griffin stopped in front of an equally angry looking Pickett.

"You are never to pull a stunt like that with Trudie again," he said quietly and calmly.

Too calmly for my tastes. I knew what that voice meant. Griffin was already kind of suspended. The last thing we needed was for him to get fired because he punched a fellow detective in the face.

"I am investigating a murder," Pickett hissed. "Considering your relationship to Ramos I would think that you would be fine with any and all techniques I use to solve it."

"I am," ground out Griffin. "But throwing Trudie into a room with your number one suspect is never going to happen again. Try solving this case with proper detective work, not cheap stunts."

Despite trying to hide it, I could see Pickett wince at the insult.

With that, Griffin grabbed my hand and we walked out. I saw Fletchall smiling as we strode by. He had seen Griffin's words with Pickett and I could tell whose side he was on.

Driving home, I noted the pensive look on Griffin's face.

"Are you okay?" I asked him gently.

"Not really. You seem to have become the focus of a suspected murderer and that does cause me some concern."

I could understand why that was.

"Also, the fact that a fellow detective was so willing to throw you into that situation makes me a little upset."

"But to clarify, I personally haven't done anything to make you mad?"

Griffin smiled tightly. "No, in this situation you haven't done anything which has caused me to be annoyed."

"Good," I said. "I think we should focus on that fact because it happens so rarely."

Griffin chuckled.

"When did you know what Pickett had done?" I asked.

"About twenty seconds before I opened the door," Griffin replied.

"This suspension could go on for a long time, couldn't it?"

"It could," Griffin conceded. "If it goes on too long I'll ask Cooper for a job."

I almost choked. There was no way that Travis would ever give Griffin a job. They may have patched things up between them but I think working together would be a step too far for everyone involved.

Griffin gave me a sideways glance. "I was joking."

Oh, thank goodness. I was used to negotiating tricky situations but I had no idea how I would have sorted that one out.

"I had a bit of a word with Fletchall about being around the bachelorette party," Griffin continued.

"What did he say?"

"According to Fletchall, before Pickett found the link with Vale, there was a theory that Jolena wasn't the primary target. They thought maybe Ramos was in danger."

"He was there to protect Ramos?"

Griffin nodded. "That scenario isn't looking very likely now that we know about Vale's history with Jolena but earlier today it was a very real fear."

"I guess that explains it," I said, a bit distractedly.

Griffin glanced over at me. "What's wrong?"

"Something's not feeling right," I said. "I just don't see Vale killing Jolena. According to him, they broke up when they were in high school. He said he wasn't overly happy with the fact she got involved with Ash because he knows how lousy Ash is with women, but he wasn't jealous."

"Of course he's going to say that," Griffin said gently. "He knew that Pickett was watching every word he said to you. It is a strong possibility that everything he said was a lie to bolster his defense."

I looked out of the car window. Griffin was probably right but there was still a part of me that was having trouble believing in Vale's guilt.

"Is the search finished at the mansion?" I asked.

"Yes," Griffin said distractedly. "From what I heard,

the band is staying in a hotel at the moment so the place is empty, but the search has finished."

"So I can go and feed the goat tomorrow morning?"

"You're really going to feed that goat for him?"

"Nobody else is at the mansion. From what I know about the other guys, none of them would have even thought about Buddy when they got out of there."

"Don't you hate that goat?"

"It's more a case of mutual loathing," I said. "But I'm not going to neglect it just because I don't like it."

"Fine," said Griffin. "Tomorrow morning we go feed the goat."

Chapter Twenty-Two

As I juggled my coffee and purse the next morning, Griffin came out of the bedroom frowning down at his phone.

"What's going on?" I asked.

"Just got a text from Ramos. It's a bit garbled. Almost sounds like she's drunk."

"Have you tried calling her?" I asked, the concern evident in my voice.

"Yeah, keeps going through to her voicemail."

"She wasn't drinking much yesterday, but I guess she could have started after she went home." I chewed my bottom lip. "You need to check on her. She made a comment yesterday about her head not being in the right place. Maybe she did something she shouldn't have."

Griffin's phone went off again and he looked down. "I think you're right. She sounds like she's in trouble. She's asking me to meet her."

"I think that would be a good idea."

"Are you going to be okay?" Griffin stopped me by putting a hand on my arm, his eyes full of concern.

I nodded. "The band isn't at the mansion. Vale's in custody. The place will be quiet and Jorge will probably get there early today. He always does. I'm going to feed Buddy and then I am going to come home and speak to Monique about this job and maybe having a bit of a break for a while. I'm going to see if I can get one of the easy jobs next time. Lord knows, I think I've earned it."

Griffin smiled. "I think that's a great idea."

"I'll meet you back here in a couple of hours and we'll get ready for the wedding," I said.

"Yes," Griffin said distractedly, frowning at the messages that seemed to be coming through on his phone.

"Something is wrong here. She sounds…lost."

I looked over the messages that were coming through. "You need to go to her now," I said firmly. "I had a feeling she was coping with everything too well. You guys are so stoic all the time that the rest of us forget that you are still human. Just take care of her. If you can't make it to the wedding, I'll give your apologies."

"I'm not standing you up for a wedding," Griffin said firmly.

I waved my hand around. "As of yesterday there was only a fifty-fifty chance that the wedding was actually going to happen. I might just end up with a day picking up the pieces with Crystal."

Griffin grabbed his jacket and gave me a quick kiss. "I'll try to be back as soon as I can," he said.

"Don't worry if you can't," I said. "Ramos needs to come first today. I'll deal with everything else."

As I drove to the mansion I felt tense with worry. Ramos seemed to be copping so many hits lately. I knew Griffin wanted to be there for her but was feeling helpless and that was never something he coped with well. Like so many men, he was a fixer. There was a problem so there had to be a solution. Unfortunately, regardless of what Pickett and Fletchall discovered, there was no fix for this situation.

As I pulled up at the front entrance the security guys at the gate waved me through.

"Everything okay?" I asked as I showed my ID like I had every day for the last month.

"All quiet," the security guard said. "You're the first one to arrive. Cops have finished and everyone left yesterday. Word is they'll be coming back later today or maybe tomorrow. Why are you here?"

"Did anyone by any chance take the goat with them?" I asked.

"There's a goat here?" chimed in the other security guard.

That comment filled me with confidence. Obviously the job description for security guard at the entrance literally meant just the entrance.

"The drummer's goat. I just need to feed it."

"Not a problem," said the guard as he opened the gate and waved me through.

With any luck I'd be able to get work done and get out of here in no time at all, ready to tackle the disaster that I was pretty sure Roxy's wedding was going to be.

Chapter Twenty-Three

I cursed roundly as I looked down at an empty pen.

"I hate you, you stupid goat. You know that, don't you?" I called out in frustration.

I had just wanted to feed the damn goat. All my hopes of this being an easy morning went flying out of the window.

I took in a deep breath. I had dealt with the antics of Hollywood divas, lecherous husbands, spoiled pop brats and directors with no self-awareness without coming unglued. I was not going to be beaten by a goat. I just needed to go looking for him again. I went around to all of the doors on the mansion only to find that they had all been locked. That was going to be a problem when I needed to start working but for now I was going to count my blessings. The thought of what Buddy could have done to the interior of that house overnight with nobody to stop him didn't bear thinking about. That meant he must still be outside. That limited the damage he could possibly do. At least I hoped it did.

I gave a cursory look of the grounds. I needed to be smart about this. The last time he had gone missing overnight I had found him by the lake. I figured that was a logical place to start looking for him. If he had been frolicking all night long, it was safe to assume that he would be thirsty. The early morning chill brought to mind the last time I had gone looking for Buddy by the lake and I shivered involuntarily. In that moment I wished Griffin hadn't got that message from Ramos because I think I would have felt a lot better with him by my side.

As I got closer to the lake I noticed what looked like a lump lying next to the shore. Feeling my heart rush into my throat, I raced over. I dropped to my knees and turned what I could see was a body over. I reared back when I saw who it was.

"Oh my God, Vale," I said as I shook his shoulders. "Wake up."

I put my ear to his chest and was reassured when I heard the steady thump of his heart. I could also see his chest rising with every breath. I shook him harder. "Vale, wake up. You need to wake up now."

I reached blindly for my purse and was stopped when a hand clamped around my wrist. I looked up in shock to see Detective Fletchall holding onto my arm.

"Thank goodness you're here," I said. "Something is wrong with Vale. We need to get an ambulance for him straight away."

Fletchall let go of my arm, kicked my bag into the water and pulled out his gun and pointed it at me.

"I don't think so. I put in a great deal of effort to put this little scene together. I really don't want anyone walking in here until I've finished it."

I stood up slowly, struggling to comprehend what was actually happening here.

"What's going on?" I asked, hearing the fear in my voice.

"I need you to help me finalize this case," Fletchall said with a small smile on his face.

"We need to get an ambulance for Vale."

"He's fine," Fletchall said dismissively. "He'll wake up in a few hours with absolutely no memory of what happened here. Rohypnol is a very useful drug sometimes."

"You gave him Rohypnol?" I gasped.

Fletchall chuckled. "You know all those warnings we give people about not accepting drinks from strangers. Seems people forget it when a cop offers them an open bottle of water during an interrogation."

I had a sinking feeling in my stomach when I remembered my pathetic gratitude for a coffee the day of my own interview.

"I thought Vale was still supposed to be in custody," I said slowly, hoping to distract him from the undeniable fact that we were alone, he was holding a gun on me and he had roofied the prime suspect in a murder case.

"Technically he was released from custody after his interview," Fletchall said. "He had a little trouble leaving the station as the drug hit his system a bit quicker than I was planning, so I helped him out. I know where all the cameras in the precinct are so I was able to bring him here without anyone being any the wiser. Getting in here was even easier. I have to say that the security on this property is really not what I would have expected."

"You came in through the back gate, didn't you?" I murmured, remembering Griffin telling me how easy it was to enter the premises. I suddenly felt sick as things started falling into place.

Fletchall nodded.

"It wasn't the first time you came in here, was it?" I asked.

"You know, people talk about you around the precinct. You have quite the reputation. Most of it is that you fall into these cases out of dumb luck. I think it may be a bit more than that."

"How did you find it the first time?" I asked, hoping that my fears weren't about to be realized.

"Why, I followed Jolena through it," he said.

In that moment I looked into his eyes and saw a hint of something that I had missed previously. It wasn't any comfort to me that it seemed everybody else had missed it too.

"It was you who killed Jolena, wasn't it?"

"Smart, I can see why Griffin is so taken with you. Took you a while to put it together though."

He was right. I wished I'd put it together an hour ago when I was safely in the arms of my boyfriend who carried a gun and had the will to use it to protect me.

"Griffin is right behind me, you know," I said, trying to bluff my way to safety.

Fletchall chuckled. "Nice try, Trudie. Griffin isn't anywhere near here. The message I sent to him took care of that."

"But it was Ramos…" my voice trailed off as I remembered that the last time I saw Ramos she had been looking for her missing phone.

"You girls weren't really paying that much attention to your surroundings last night, were you? You probably should be more alert when you're out in public. All manner of things can happen when you're not paying attention. For example, a phone can go missing and be used the next morning to distract the one person I don't want to be involved in this scenario."

"Why are you doing this?"

"Do you know what it's like to truly love someone and know that they will never love you back?"

I shook my head.

"The day Liza Ramos walked into the precinct I knew that I was never going to love another woman. She didn't even look in my direction. The only time she would speak to me was when I did something or said something to annoy her so we ended up with this strange, combative relationship. It wasn't what I wanted but as long as I could be around her I was satisfied. I tried to get involved with other women but they could never compare to her."

I waited as he seemed lost in his memories, my eyes casting around as I desperately tried to work out what my options were.

"I've been following Liza's partners around for months. All I've been doing is making sure they were good enough for her."

Fletchall looked at me expectantly as if hoping that I would recognize the sacrifices he had been making for the love of his life. He was definitely looking in the wrong direction. I was firmly of the opinion that if someone didn't love you, then it wasn't worth fighting for them. Life was too short to hold out for the impossible.

"I knew about the incident with Jolena, here with Ash. She had the woman that I loved and she was throwing it away. She was going to break Liza's heart and I couldn't allow that to happen. It made me sick the way she was acting at the barbecue, as if the two of them had this wonderful relationship. I knew Jolena would cheat on Liza again at the first chance she had. I was right, wasn't I?" he said triumphantly. "She came here that night, looking to meet up with Ash again."

I didn't move or say a word. There was no way that I wanted to aggravate what was already a seriously messed up situation.

"I followed Jolena here and saw her sneak in through the gate in the back wall. I knew she was going to meet up with Ash again. I couldn't allow that to happen. I couldn't let her keep making a fool out of Liza. Not when I had the power to prevent it."

Fletchall looked out over the lake. "You should have seen her face when she saw me." He chuckled. "She tried to bluff her way out of it at first. She thought I was an idiot who couldn't possibly know what she had been doing. I knew though and I had to stop her. She wasn't good enough for Liza and she was never going to be."

Fletchall took in a deep breath. "Maybe I shouldn't have done it."

That surprised me. A moment of sanity from the man who was clearly not operating on all cylinders. Maybe I could work with that.

He shook his head. "But it's done now and I need to make sure they never work out that it was me that did it. That's why I need your help."

Obviously, if he was thinking I would be helping him, the moment of sanity was well and truly over.

"How do you want me to help?" I asked quietly, hoping to delay him. It wouldn't take Griffin long to work out that something wasn't right. All I had to do was keep him talking long enough for that to happen. Maybe I would be able to talk Fletchall out of making a huge mistake. That was Plan A. Rescue by Griffin was Plan B. At least my brain had unfrozen enough to start making plans.

"I had originally intended for Ash to take the fall for Jolena's death but he was just too obvious."

That was true. Ash had been my number one pick and I'm pretty sure he had been on top of everyone's list. Some people just live a life that screams that, yes, they could be a potential murderer. Ash fitted into that thinking very nicely.

"That's the trick when trying to find someone to take the fall for a crime. Most people who try to frame somebody leave too much evidence, like they are trying to create a huge neon sign telling the police to look here. Too much evidence is just as much of a problem as too little evidence. It just doesn't feel right. But then I found out how Vale had been Jolena's boyfriend in high school. That was an obscure enough connection that it seemed much more believable as a killer. Especially as Ash so obviously didn't seem to care one way or the other about Jolena. Jealousy is always a prime motivator. I just needed to make sure Pickett found Jolena's necklace in Vale's room as a trophy. His fight with Ash over you was like a gift. Everything he did just seemed to point towards him."

That was all very interesting but I still didn't know why I was standing next to the lake in the early morning with a psychopathic stalker and an unconscious drummer.

"Why am I here?" I asked in a subdued voice.

Fletchall grimaced. "See, the thing is that even though we have circumstantial evidence against Vale, it really isn't enough for a conviction. Maybe if he was poor and only had access to a really bad lawyer, then maybe, we could get a conviction. But he isn't. He has the money and the means to get this case tossed out of court in a heartbeat.

What we need to really make this case stick is if we had a second murder case against him. One which even the best of defense lawyers wouldn't be able to dispute."

My stomach dropped as I had a very bad feeling where this was going.

Fletchall's expression was almost sympathetic. "I'm sorry, Trudie. I really am. If there was a way for me to do this without you being involved I would have taken it. But Vale has taken a liking to you. This wouldn't work with anyone else. You are the perfect victim for him. He's got feelings for you but you're involved with Griffin. You reject him and he can't handle it. Everyone knows about the fight earlier. This won't come as a true surprise when looking at it in that context. And once we have your death to link it too, the police won't look anywhere else for Jolena's killer. Especially as I will be leading up the investigation. Don't worry, Trudie. Justice will be done and your murder will be solved."

"Your partner may not look at it that way," I said desperately. "You are not taking into account that he's going to look into this further."

"Pickett is useless," Fletchall snorted derisively. "He couldn't find a murderer in a prison yard."

I really hoped that wasn't true because at this moment I was thinking that Pickett being on the case was my best chance at justice.

"Griffin won't let this go," I warned. "If anything happens to me, he will not leave any stone unturned to make sure that the real murderer is caught. You will never be able to rest. You will never be safe."

"Normally I would agree with you. But I have a feeling that losing you will put Griffin off his game for a very long time. He already has reason to suspect Vale. Anger and grief will take care of the rest."

Fletchall holstered his weapon and I had a sudden burst of hope.

"I'm truly sorry, Trudie," he said regretfully and that

small flame of hope died.

In a blinding flash of insight I knew what he was going to do. He couldn't afford to shoot me. Despite the fact we were right at the back of the property, too far for people at the front of the property to hear my scream, a gunshot would alert security. Whatever way Fletchall was planning to stage this scene was going to take time, time he wouldn't have if security came running. Also, a bullet could be linked back to him. That didn't fit in with his master plan. No, Detective Marty Fletchall was going to strangle me to death, just like he did Jolena. He was then going to toss my lifeless body into the lake. I could see the whole thing running through my head like a macabre thriller movie.

Looks like I was going to go with Plan C, as in fighting with everything I had. I had no illusions about my chances of fighting Fletchall off. He was a big man and looked like he had gone a few rounds with criminals of every persuasion. I was a personal assistant who preferred my violence in an action film, on a movie screen. I couldn't watch a lot of the newer television shows because I found them too violent and gory. But I had a choice to make. If he did manage to kill me than I wanted so much DNA under my fingernails that they would come looking for him the second they managed to analyze it. I also had a bit more faith in Pickett than Fletchall obviously had.

Fletchall took a step towards me and I took a step back. The fact that I had obviously made the decision to fight him didn't seem to be relaying to the rest of my body. My fight or flight response had obviously come down firmly in the flight camp. I didn't think that was going to help me either. Out of the corner of my eye I saw a blur of gray and white. I froze on the spot and my mouth dropped open when I saw Fletchall get knocked off his feet by the same goat that I had been roundly cursing for the past several days. Fletchall fell into the lake and Buddy bleated at him triumphantly.

"You stupid son of a…" Fletchall growled as he pulled his gun.

"I really wouldn't do that if I were you," said Detective Pickett as he walked out into the open with his gun pointed directly at the soaked detective.

I really hoped that this meant that I was safe, although considering how my morning had been going, I wasn't confident of it.

"Are you okay, Miss Eyre?"

"I don't know yet," I said. "Am I okay?"

Pickett threw a glance in my direction. "As long as you didn't have anything to do with the murder of Jolena Aaron, you are completely safe from me."

I was grateful for the reassurance.

"Toss the gun, Fletchall," Pickett returned his attention to the real threat of the day.

Fletchall looked down at the gun in his hand. I held my breath.

"Don't be more of an idiot than you already have been."

I could see that negotiating was not part of Pickett's skill set.

Fletchall cursed again and threw the gun to the side. At some point, someone was going to need to go swimming to get that gun back, as well as my purse.

"Now walk out of the water with your hands up. Do not make any sudden moves or I will shoot you."

I believed every word that he said. I stepped back to get as far away from Fletchall as I possibly could and bumped into Buddy. He bleated at me indignantly and for the first time I didn't mind. I knelt down and put my arms around his neck.

"Thank you," I murmured.

"You know I actually had a part in saving you," Pickett said as he put handcuffs on Fletchall.

"Not until after Buddy saved me," I said as I was stroking Buddy's head.

"How's the drummer?" Pickett asked as he pushed Fletchall to sit on the ground with his hands behind his back.

I reached over and put my hand on Vale's chest. His heart was beating strongly.

"How long does it take Rohypnol to wear off?" I asked.

"Usually a few hours. I'll get an ambulance."

Pickett pulled out a phone and, while keeping an eye on Fletchall, started making calls. When he finished he looked over at me.

"Seriously, are you okay? Did he hurt you in any way?"

I shook my head. "I'll be having nightmares for a very long time but he didn't technically hurt me. Not that I'm not completely grateful, because I am, but what are you doing here?"

"I'm Internal Affairs. I've been investigating Detective Fletchall here."

I didn't know who was more surprised to hear that, me or Fletchall.

"You knew he was a killer?" I asked incredulously.

"No," Pickett admitted. "We've been investigating him for some inconsistencies in cases throughout his career. His old partner on the Vice squad got pulled in for illegal behavior and he's been implicating Fletchall in some of his less than savory activities. I was sent in undercover to see what I could find out."

"So you had no idea he was a killer?"

Pickett shook his head. "No, but the thought that a corrupt cop took that final step to the dark side isn't really a big jump. His behavior during this investigation has been a bit off and even a moron like me was able to pick up on it."

He had obviously been around long enough to hear Fletchall's assessment of his detective abilities, which brought me to the next question. "How long have you been here?"

"I saw him assisting Vale out of the station and decided to follow."

"So you've been here the entire time. You knew that he was going to kill me and you let this situation keep going. Do you know how scared I was? Why didn't you arrest him earlier?"

Pickett indicated the body camera on his jacket. "I needed him to implicate himself. The evidence against him for Jolena's murder is pretty much non-existent. Without that confession to you, I had nothing. The more he talked, the tighter the case became. Do you really want him walking around the streets again?"

I had to admit I didn't. That still didn't stop me from disliking Detective Pickett a great deal.

Chapter Twenty-Four

I raised my head as I heard sirens blaring in the distance. An ambulance and police cars were heading our way. I looked down at Buddy and I didn't know whether it was the life and death situation we had found ourselves in but we had bonded. It was through that bond I could tell he had had enough and wanted to go somewhere safe.

"Can I put Buddy back in his pen?" I asked. "I think all these people are going to freak him out."

Pickett looked surprised. "You've been held by a murderer, threatened with a horrifying death, one of your clients is currently unconscious on the ground and you are worried about the psychological trauma that a goat is going through?"

"That goat saved my life while you hid behind a tree with an ulterior motive. Frankly, until ten minutes ago I hated this goat, but now, I like him more than I like you."

Pickett shrugged. "Take the goat to his pen but you need to come right back here because you and I are going to be having a talk down at the station."

Of course we were, because everything in my life ended up with me sitting in an interrogation room.

After I'd finished making Buddy as comfortable as a hero could be, I returned to the lake to find that Vale had found his way to consciousness and was lying on a gurney about to be loaded into an ambulance. He stopped the paramedics and waved me over. As I reached him, he gripped my hand.

"The cop told me what happened. Are you okay?"

I nodded. "How about you?"

Vale gave me a crooked smile. "As well as I can be considering I had my drink spiked by the cop who was trying to frame me for murder."

"Yeah, it's been quite the morning," I said.

Vale squeezed my hand. "I'm sorry I've made your life uncomfortable. I knew you had a boyfriend but I kind of liked you. I'm so used to getting what I wanted these days that I figured I could have you too. I shouldn't have done that. If I had just left you alone you would never have been pulled into this mess."

He looked so downcast that I felt sorry for him. "I'm fine. Everything worked out in the end and the important thing is that Jolena is going to get justice. Thanks to this morning's effort, Fletchall will be going away for a very long time."

The paramedic stepped up. "I'm sorry Ma'am but we're going to need to get the patient to hospital."

I nodded, squeezed Vale's hand and stepped back.

As I watched the ambulance drive off I felt Detective Pickett step up behind me. "I need you to come with me to the station," he said. "Griffin's been notified and he's going to meet us there. Seems he was already on his way."

Seems like Plan B would have worked as well if I'd just been able to keep Fletchall talking for long enough.

As soon as we arrived at the station Pickett deposited me in the interview room. For the first time I only waited a few minutes before the door opened again and Pickett walked in. He put a cup of coffee in front of me and I don't think I hid my expression of distaste very well.

"Just coffee, nothing else," he murmured.

"I think I'm going to have a little problem with anything a police officer gives me at the moment. Might take me a little while to get over it." I pushed the cup away. "Is this going to take long? I have a wedding to go to."

"That will be a change of pace for the day."

"Yes. A couple of hours ago a wedding was the absolute last thing that I felt like doing. Now, I'm kind of grateful that I'm going to get the chance to go."

"I can imagine. Detective Griffin told me that you saw

Fletchall following you last night."

"It might not have been me, it could have been Ramos," I pointed out.

"It could have been. Fletchall's not talking at all so there is a chance we may never know. It does look like he stole Ramos's phone at one of those two venues. He used that to lure Griffin away so that you would be alone when you got to the mansion."

"Worked a treat, didn't it?" I said.

Pickett inclined his head. "The case we're putting together looks like classic stalker material. Rationality left the building long ago but he's still a cop. He was using those skills to build the best case possible against Vale. Might have worked too if the goat hadn't got involved."

"Don't sell yourself short," I said sarcastically. "I'm sure you would have come out and arrested him at some point. I like to believe that it would be before I was killed."

Pickett looked at me sourly. "Of course I would have."

I wasn't so convinced. It could just have been the trauma but I was not so sure Detective Pickett would have risked his investigation just to save little old me.

"Why did you go down to the lake this morning?" Picket asked.

"Buddy was missing again. The last time he got out of his pen he ended up at the lake…" My voice tapered off. "I told Fletchall that at the first interview. That's the exact same thing that happened the morning I found Jolena's body."

"Probably where he got the idea to lure you down there. He let the goat out of the pen and human nature would dictate that you would go looking for the goat at the place you found him the last time he went missing."

"It was a great plan, wasn't it?"

"Nobody said Fletchall was dumb. The man is pretty intelligent, if you don't take into account his willingness to coldly kill a woman to frame someone else for the murder he had previously committed."

My stomach was not reacting well to this information.

"Can we finish up soon? I'm starting to feel a bit ill."

For the first time, Pickett looked sympathetic. "Sure."

He led me out of the interview room and I was faced with Griffin who was standing as close to the doorway as he possibly could without blocking it. He pulled me into his arms and the knot in my stomach started to calm down.

"Tell me you're okay," he whispered into my hair. "I just need to know that you're okay."

I nodded. "I'll be fine. I just need you to hold me for a little bit longer."

"I can do that," he said.

"Trudie can go home," Pickett said from somewhere behind me.

Griffin didn't say anything. He just gathered me close and led me out to the car. I didn't say a word as we drove home but I could feel Griffin glancing at me with a worried expression on his face.

As he closed the door to my apartment I turned to him, buried my head in his chest and started crying.

"Oh, honey," he soothed as he stroked a hand gently up and down my back.

"I just need a moment," I said between sobs. "I just need to let this out."

"It's okay, take as long as you like."

Griffin picked me up as though I weighed nothing and took me over to the couch. He sat down with me still in his arms and muttered nonsensical things to me as I calmed down.

"You're safe now. He can't hurt you."

"I know, I've just never been that scared in my life. I've been in some bad situations but that was terrifying. I honestly thought he was going to kill me in a horrible, horrible way and there was nothing I could do."

"I wish I'd been there. I wish I could have stopped it."

Griffin's eyes were tortured and I knew for a man like

him this would have been seen as a failure.

"None of us knew. For goodness sake, I invited the man in for a coffee. I thought he was nice."

I really needed to work on my instincts because if this situation had proved anything it was that they were absolutely useless.

I used the palms of my hands to wipe my eyes and took in a deep breath. "Okay, I'm fine and we have a wedding to go to."

Griffin looked stunned. "You can't be serious. We are not still going to that wedding, are we?"

"Absolutely," I said with a watery smile. "If there was ever a wedding that was going to self-destruct, this is it. I wouldn't put it past John's daughters to stage an intervention to stop this thing. Crystal may need back up and if things go really bad we may need your badge."

"Fine, but the second it starts looking like it's too much, I am taking you out of there."

"Deal," I said. "As long as we wait until after the vows have been said."

I spent extra time getting myself ready for the wedding and by the time I finished I had convinced myself that I had managed to hide the damage from my meltdown.

"You ready?" Griffin called from the living room.

"Uh huh," I called back as I grabbed my clutch, although I no longer had a purse or phone as it was now being examined by forensics thanks to Fletchall kicking it into the water. I wasn't really sure what my waterlogged possessions were going to add to the case against him but Pickett had insisted.

"Wow," whistled Griffin. "You look gorgeous."

I smiled shyly. "You look pretty good yourself."

He did. I always thought that Griffin in jeans looked amazing but when he wore a suit, he took my breath away.

A serious look came over Griffin's face. "Trudie…"

We were interrupted by Griffin's phone ringing, as so often happened in our relationship.

"Timing," he muttered as he looked down at the screen. "It's the lieutenant. I'll be just a second."

He walked into the bedroom. I could hear his voice rising and when he hung up I heard words that I usually didn't hear coming from Griffin.

"They want you to go in, don't they?" I said when he joined me in the living room.

"Yeah," he replied. "I'm quite happy to tell them where to stick it this time. But they want to talk to me about Fletchall. I don't want to risk someone dropping the ball and him not getting everything that he deserves."

I shook my head. "No, of course not."

"I will be as quick as I possibly can and I'll join you at the wedding," he promised. He bent his head and gave me a quick kiss before heading out the door.

Chapter Twenty-Five

I sat down on the couch. I really didn't want to go to this wedding. What I wanted was to curl up in bed and hide from the world for a while. With Griffin here I had been able to push myself into believing I could do this. Now that I was going to have to turn up to the wedding alone, I wasn't too keen on the idea. I debated with myself for several minutes as I tried to convince myself to get going. The internal argument was interrupted by a knock on my door. I opened it to find Miss Betsy standing there.

"Your man asked me if I could take you to the wedding."

I should have expected Griffin to do something thoughtful to take care of me.

"Something bad has happened, hasn't it?" Miss Betsy said.

I nodded, trying really hard to control the tears I could feel crowding into my eyes again.

"Are you going to be okay or do I need to pull you out of this?" she asked.

"I'll be fine," I smiled tremulously. "I just got a really big scare. I never want to feel that terrified again in my life."

"But you survived," Miss Betsy said. "That is what matters, the fact that you got to come home. Everything else you can deal with."

She was right. I could always count on Miss Betsy to go straight to the heart of a situation.

As I got into her car Miss Betsy grinned, "I knew something bad had happened. That man has got access to my driving record. No way would he normally entrust the most precious thing in his life to my driving skills."

I laughed just as she'd wanted.

"That's better. Now I suggest you hang on. I want to get to this wedding on time. After yesterday I'm curious to see whether it is actually going to happen."

From long experience I knew to do as I was told. The wedding was being held in the garden of a friend of John's with a marquee set up for the reception. Considering the short amount of time that had been available for planning, everything looked beautiful.

"I guess all that experience had to be good for something," muttered Miss Betsy.

I had to stop myself from laughing. I spotted Edwin over in the corner, looking concerned, and tugged Miss Betsy behind me.

"What's going on?" I asked.

"There's going to be a bit of a delay with the ceremony," he said diplomatically.

"This sounds good," Miss Betsy said eagerly. "What happened? The daughters chained themselves to their father's car, didn't they? They had the looks of the kind of people who'd do that."

Edwin didn't smile at what I thought was an obvious joke. "As far as I know there haven't been any chains. There has been some yelling, some threats and a huge amount of emotional blackmail. Roxy's a mess and Crystal is trying to deal with her."

"What are the odds of this wedding actually happening?" asked Miss Betsy with what I considered an inappropriate look of glee on her face.

Edwin shrugged his shoulders. "I wouldn't be betting on it. John's son looks like he could go either way but his daughters are raising holy hell. Depends on how much he wants to marry Roxy I guess."

An hour later we discovered that John really wanted to marry Roxy. So much so that he was willing to have his daughters walk out of his wedding if that was the only way for the day to go forward. A part of me had to admire that kind of determination. I just hoped that Roxy proved to have some staying power this time to reward that kind of faith.

Despite everyone's fears that Megan and Sally would abandon the wedding, they proved themselves by standing next to their father, albeit with disapproving frowns instead of the traditional smiles.

When the minister asked if there were any objections, there was an audible intake of breath around the room. Realizing the precariousness of the situation the minister rushed on, barely giving anyone the time to think, let alone object.

I looked up as Griffin slid into the seat next to me.

"Am I too late?" he asked.

I shook my head. We sat there quietly even though I was dying to ask what had happened. As Roxy and John recited their loving vows, with their respective children glaring at each other, I felt Griffin's hand cover mine as he entwined our fingers.

I smiled at the scene in front of me. If you could ignore the obvious tension in the room, the day was proving to be quite romantic.

When the ceremony was finished and the party started there was a noticeable easing of hostilities. Of course, that was being helped along by Miss Betsy plying Megan and Sally with a steady stream of alcohol to improve their spirits.

When the music started I dragged Griffin up on the dance floor. Swaying to the music I laid my head against his chest.

"Crystal and her mom look like they are going well," muttered Griffin.

I smiled as I saw the two women laughing.

"Goes to show, you should never write anyone off. People constantly surprise you," I said. "How are things at the station?"

Griffin smiled humorlessly. "The lieutenant's losing it a bit. He's having to explain how he managed to have a homicidal stalker as one of his detectives and never saw it coming. To be perfectly fair though, none of us saw it coming. We all knew that Fletchall was a bit on the sleazy side but this…this was unexpected."

"How's Ramos doing?"

Griffin sighed. "She's not doing well. She wants a transfer and at this stage the department is willing to let her do anything that she wants. For that matter, some of the legal bigwigs at the department have been indicating that you would be able to launch a lawsuit if you were so inclined. If there is anything you want, this is the moment to ask for it."

"Does she still blame me?" I whispered. Our relationship had never been good but I had a feeling it would never recover from this.

Griffin smiled sadly. "I don't think she really blames you. You just might be collateral damage. I think most of us are. She just wants to get away from what is an ugly situation."

"So what happens to you?" I asked.

"My unofficial suspension is over and I am now partnered with former Internal Affairs Detective Desmond Pickett. That's going to be fun. The guy's a bit uptight."

A bark of laughter shot out of me. "You're complaining about someone being uptight. Do you have any idea how many people tell me that about you?"

"Yes, well, it seems I'm now considered a bit of a loose cannon according to Lieutenant Ellis and he's putting the blame for that completely on you."

I grimaced. "I seem to be having a very bad influence on the people in his department. I can almost understand that attitude."

Griffin raised his hand and stroked down the side of my cheek. "I wouldn't have it any other way," he whispered.

I smiled up at him.

Griffin looked down at me and I could see a tenseness

to him.

"What's wrong?" I asked.

"Marry me," he said, and as usual with Griffin it was more of a statement than a question.

My jaw dropped. "Are you serious?" I asked.

Griffin nodded. "I've known that you were the one for me from that moment when you saved Sean from the mobsters on our first case. I remember hearing you walk into that room to save a sixteen year old boy getting a bullet in the brain and thinking that one day I was going to marry you."

Not the most romantic of proposals but if it had been, it wouldn't have been Griffin. He wasn't about romantic words but then neither was I.

"Marry me," repeated Griffin. "I swear I will do everything in my power to make sure you are happy and loved for the rest of your life."

I didn't hesitate. I loved Jake Griffin and I couldn't think of anything that I would rather do than spend the rest of my life with him.

I nodded. "Yes," I said, wrapped my arms around his neck and kissed him.

About The Author

Leonie Gant started her writing career at the age of ten when she stuffed notes in her pencil case full of ideas for mysteries that Nancy Drew and the Hardy Boys should really have been solving. After years of watching mysteries play out in her head, she decided that writing them down was the best way to deal with them.

In her life away from writing, she is a voracious reader with not nearly enough time to make her way through all the books that she wants to read. She enjoys bushwalking, sewing and chocolate, possibly not in that order. She also believes in the value of trying new things, walking in the rain and enjoying every moment.

To find out more about Leonie Gant and her books
www.leoniegant.com

Discover other titles by Leonie Gant
Not Famous in Hollywood
Not Happily Married in Hollywood
Not Talented in Hollywood
Not Wanted in Hollywood
Not Forgotten in Hollywood

www.ingramcontent.com/pod-product-compliance
Lightning Source LLC
Chambersburg PA
CBHW020410150626
46554CB00012B/549